Other books by this author available
from New English Library:

EDGE 1: THE LONER
EDGE 2: TEN THOUSAND DOLLARS AMERICAN
EDGE 3: APACHE DEATH
EDGE 4: KILLER'S BREED
EDGE 5: BLOOD ON SILVER
EDGE 6: THE BLUE, THE GREY AND THE RED
EDGE 7: CALIFORNIA KILLING
EDGE 8: SEVEN OUT OF HELL
EDGE 9: BLOODY SUMMER
EDGE 10: VENGEANCE IS BLACK
EDGE 11: SIOUX UPRISING
EDGE 12: THE BIGGEST BOUNTY
EDGE 13: A TOWN CALLED HATE
EDGE 14: THE BIG GOLD
EDGE 15: BLOOD RUN
EDGE 16: THE FINAL SHOT
EDGE 17: VENGEANCE VALLEY
EDGE 18: TEN TOMBSTONES TO TEXAS
EDGE 19: ASHES AND DUST
EDGE 20: SULLIVAN'S LAW
EDGE 21: RHAPSODY IN RED
EDGE 22: SLAUGHTER ROAD
EDGE 23: ECHOES OF WAR
EDGE 24: THE DAY DEMOCRACY DIED
EDGE 25: VIOLENCE TRAIL
EDGE 26: SAVAGE DAWN
EDGE 27: DEATH DRIVE
EDGE 28: EVE OF EVIL
EDGE 29: THE LIVING, THE DYING AND THE DEAD
EDGE 30: WAITING FOR A TRAIN
EDGE 31: THE GUILTY ONES
EDGE 32: THE FRIGHTENED GUN

ADAM STEELE 1: THE VIOLENT PEACE
ADAM STEELE 2: BOUNTY HUNTER
ADAM STEELE 3: HELL'S JUNCTION
ADAM STEELE 4: VALLEY OF BLOOD
ADAM STEELE 5: GUN RUN
ADAM STEELE 6: THE KILLING ART
ADAM STEELE 7: CROSS-FIRE
ADAM STEELE 8: COMANCHE CARNAGE
ADAM STEELE 9: BADGE IN THE DUST
ADAM STEELE 10: THE LOSERS
ADAM STEELE 11: LYNCH TOWN
ADAM STEELE 12: DEATH TRAIL
ADAM STEELE 13: BLOODY BORDER
ADAM STEELE 14: DELTA DUEL
ADAM STEELE 15: RIVER OF DEATH
ADAM STEELE 16: NIGHTMARE AT NOON
ADAM STEELE 17: SATAN'S DAUGHTERS
ADAM STEELE 18: THE HARD WAY
ADAM STEELE 19: THE TARNISHED STAR
ADAM STEELE 20: WANTED FOR MURDER
ADAM STEELE 21: WAGONS EAST
ADAM STEELE 22: THE BIG GAME
ADAM STEELE 23: FORT DESPAIR

THE HATED
George G. Gilman

NEW ENGLISH LIBRARY/TIMES MIRROR

For
R.H.
who once rode out to the
south-west and wore many
hats.

A New English Library Original Publication, 1979

© 1979 by George G. Gilman

First NEL paperback edition December 1979

NEL Books are published by
New English Library from
Barnard's Inn, Holborn,
London EC1N 2JR
Made and printed in Great Britain by
Hunt Barnard Printing Ltd.,
Aylesbury, Bucks.

45004336 3

Chapter One

The man called Edge had not seen another human being or even a sign of the presence of another human being for three and a half days. He was riding south down the Continental Divide towards the border of the Territory of New Mexico and the Mexican state of Chihuahua. Living frugally off the supplies he had purchased in Silver City and sleeping peacefully under the stars by night, he travelled by day at a measured pace astride a grey mare. While he was awake he constantly watched for any indication that he was not alone in this sun-bleached, hostile terrain. And even when he slept, protected from the mountain cold by his bedroll blankets, his resting mind was animalistically attuned to trigger him awake should he hear – or even sense – a stranger in the vicinity of his night camp. Waking or sleeping, prepared to meet and deal with any kind of threat: and assuming as a matter of course that every stranger was a threat.

Then, at close to noon on the fourth day out of Silver City, he saw the small huddle of buildings in the distance: at first sight distorted by the shimmering heat-haze that hung along every horizon like a slick, billowing, not quite transparent curtain. The buildings were directly on his due south path in the high, broad valley between the Hatchet Mountains to the west and the Cedars to the east. And offered a hard to resist invitation to enjoy shade and perhaps even coolness out of the direct glare of the cruelly hot sun.

He ran the back of his right hand over his forehead then dragged the palm and fingers down over his nose, cheeks and jaw. But even before he had wiped the sweat off his hand on the pants leg contouring his thigh, more beads of salty wetness had squeezed through the pores of his face.

It was either a handsome or an ugly face, depending upon how the person looking at it felt about the physical combination of features drawn from a Mexican father and a Scandinavian mother – and the more subtle coalescence of latent brutality and deep rooted melancholy that was also visible to anyone with more than a modicum of perception. His coloration was burnt brown, from the Mexican half of his parentage and a lifetime of almost forty years exposure to the elements. And the skin, stretched taut between high cheekbones and firm jawline – almost rock-like across his low forehead – was deeply furrowed by more than merely the passing of the years. These ruts in the dark brown skin providing the clue that the man's demeanour of brooding suspicion, underlying cruelty and passive sadness – camouflaged to a large extent by an almost constant mask of inscrutability – was the result of great suffering.

The predominant features of the long, lean face were the man's eyes: light blue and piercing in the way they surveyed the world from between permanently narrowed lids. The colour of ice in an Arctic sea, and for most of the time as cold-looking. His nose was hawklike and his mouthline was long, the lips thin. When these lips were drawn back in a smile which seldom, if ever, injected warmth into his eyes, the teeth were seen to be even and very white. On a day like this one, when he had shaved before leaving his night camp at dawn, a forest of dark bristles had sprouted over his lower face by noon: slightly thicker along his top lip and to either side of his mouth to suggest a Mexican-style moustache.

His face was framed by jet black hair which grew thick and long, the ends brushing his shoulders and concealing the nape of his neck.

He was a tall man – six feet three inches – and well built, with the close to two hundred pounds evenly distributed over his frame. Lean, but far from thin.

His clothing was serviceable and had provided good service. A grey cotton shirt with one pocket that bulged with the makings of cigarettes, black denim pants with the cuffs worn outside of spurless black riding boots, a grey Stetson with a wide brim and low crown and a grey kerchief tied at the back. This last item concealing a leather thong strung with faded coloured beads to which – at the nape of his neck – was attached a soft leather sheath hanging inside his shirt. In the sheath was a sharply honed straight razor which he did not reserve exclusively for shaving.

Around his waist was a scuffed leather gunbelt with the holster tied down to his right thigh. Jutting from the holster was the butt of a standard .44-40 Army Model Remington. In every loop of the gunbelt was a shell, suitable for the sixgun and for the yellow-boy Winchester which was slotted in the boot hung from the Western-style saddle on which he rode. Lashed on behind the saddle was his bedroll with a knee-length black leather coat on top.

As he rode close enough for the group of buildings to be clearly defined as a single storey adobe house and a frame barn and stable with a corral out back, Edge dug out the makings from his shirt pocket and rolled and lit a cigarette. Which he hung at the corner of his mouth: leaving both hands free to hold the reins. Lightly. Ready to reach for the Remington or the Winchester should the homestead hold a threat.

At first impression, it appeared to be abandoned: looking cheerless and uncared for under the cloudless blue dome of sky from which a fiercely hot sun relentlessly glared. The flat-roofed adobe house, longer than it was wide, faced west with a wooden stoop at the front. Out back was a yard some thirty by thirty feet with the stable directly opposite the rear of the house and a barn along the south side.

No smoke rose from a stack at a corner of the house, one of the two barn doors hung drunkenly open, wrenched free of the upper hinge, and the fencing enclosing the corral behind the stable was broken in many places and leaning over in others. The few attempts which had been made to repair ravages wrought by the elements were undertaken long ago. Timber was bleached and warped, one window which flanked the closed door of the house was boarded over and the pane in that on the other side was cracked from top to bottom. A fine layer of grey dust coated every flat surface.

But close to the homestead, within a few feet of riding his horse on to the once-cultivated front yard, Edge sensed that the place

7

was not deserted. And he became tense, poised to react to sound or movement without altering his posture astride the mare or changing a single plane in the impassive set of his face. Fully aware of his exposed position on a broad area of sparsely-vegetated terrain where the house and outbuildings provided the only substantial cover for at least a mile in any direction. Thus had his course towards the homestead always been designed to bring him close to the house at the solid, windowless north wall.

A hen clucked and the half-breed reined his mount to an abrupt halt: dropped his right hand to his thigh, two inches away from the jutting butt of the holstered Remington. His slitted eyes stared fixedly at the closed door and cracked window pane. The chicken made more clucking sounds: the kind that preceded the laying of an egg. The noise was abruptly curtailed and the scrawny-looking bird bellied out from under the stoop. And ignored the man and horse to peck at the hard-packed, unpromising-looking dirt in front of the house.

Inside the house, a woman began to sing. Her voice plaintively melancholy in the all-pervading silence which followed the end of the hen's clucking and the halting of the mare.

> *'I'll sing you a song, though it may be a sad one*
> *Of trials and troubles and where first begun*
> *I left my dear family, my friends and my home*
> *To cross the wide mountains and deserts to roam . . .'*

The door creaked open and Edge and the woman saw each other midway through the final line of the first verse. They were equally unmoved by the sight of a total stranger and the half-breed remained tense behind impassiveness while the woman completed the line without a falter and with her doleful expression unchanged.

She was a fine-looking woman of about thirty-eight or nine – Edge felt reluctant to place her at forty or above. Tall, perhaps five feet ten inches, with a full-bodied form and long, finely shaped legs contoured by a man's check shirt with the buttons in danger of popping and tight-fitting blue denim pants. She had sandy hair, cropped short, and an oval-shaped face with tanned skin, large

8

green eyes and an attractively pouting mouth.

As she stepped out from the shade of the stoop roof she swayed a little and Edge was able to make a reasonable guess at the reason for her unsteadiness from the blotch of high colour beneath the tan on each of her cheeks and the glazed quality of her eyes.

'Well, hello to you, mister,' she greeted, showing fine teeth in a bright smile of greeting. Ireland sounded in her voice, which was slurred as she spoke: totally at odds with the bitter sweetness of her tone when she had been singing.

'And to you, ma'am,' Edge responded, noting that a single plain band on the third finger of her left hand was the only jewellery she wore. Then, as he swung down from the saddle and led the mare across the front yard: 'I think maybe the hen just produced the makings of your lunch.'

'Huh?' she asked.

'The chicken just laid an egg,' the half-breed augmented.

She shifted her eyes from the man to the hen and back again, and had trouble with the change of focus.

'Eggs are lucky,' she said, her slack mouth unpainted like the rest of her face. As the smile came dangerously close to being a sneer.

'How's that, ma'am?'

'They're about all that does get laid around here, mister!' she growled. And gaped her lips wide to vent a shrieking laugh. Which lasted perhaps a full five seconds: before her big eyes rolled up in their sockets, she made a sound as if she was going to vomit, then collapsed into a drunken stupor: falling face down and spread-eagled on the rock-hard earth.

Edge took the remains of the cigarette out of the corner of his mouth, dropped it to the ground and crushed the glowing tobacco embers under a boot heel.

The mare whinnied and the chicken squawked and scampered back under the stoop boarding. As the slitted eyes of the half-breed raked over the tightly clad splayed thighs and the erotically mounded buttocks of the unconscious woman.

'Question is, lady,' he murmured as the carnal glint grew brighter in his eyes, 'right now am I a good or a bad egg?'

Chapter Two

Careful about the position of his hands, he rolled the woman over onto her back, lifted her with ease and set her down gently in the shade of the stoop roof. Then he attended to his horse, leading the mare around to the back yard and into the stable. A half-dozen other hens watched him eagerly from the threshold of the barn with the sagging door.

The stable smelled of fairly recent horse droppings and there was fresh straw in one of the ten stalls. And several bales of hay stacked against a wall, with sweet water in a trough opposite.

He unsaddled the horse and while the animal drank he prepared a stall with bedding and feed. Then, after shutting the mare in the stall, he sidetracked from his return to the front of the house to check in the barn. The chickens had a roost in one corner of the large interior. Except for a flatbed wagon – as ill cared for as the house and outbuildings – the barn was otherwise empty.

On the stoop of the house, the woman had rolled onto her side and curled up into a ball, as if she felt cold. She was snoring softly. She grunted irritably when he picked her up again, but her eyes remained firmly closed as he carried her into the house.

The air inside felt even hotter than out in the broad valley, malodorous with the mingled smells of cheap liquor, stale sweat and old cooking. The room was a big one, taking up over half the house area, and served as a parlour and kitchen. It had the advantage of the window which, although cracked, was still glazed. In addition to the front door, three others led off the room. One from the kitchen area gave on to the yard at the rear of the house. The two others were in a side wall and Edge carried the woman through that which was open into a small bedroom which admitted daylight only by way of the door from the main room and cracks around the boarded-up window. The double bed which used up most of the floor space was unmade, the linen dirty and rancid-smelling. The rest of the furniture consisted of a free-standing wardrobe and a five-drawer bureau with an attached mirror and a basin, pitcher and kerosene lamp.

As he laid the woman on her back on the bed, Edge's left boot kicked a bottle and set it rolling. It sounded empty. In the squalid, evil-smelling bedroom, any remnants of sexual desire for the full-bodied woman were dispelled from his mind. Out in the main room of the house, with the door closed on the woman, the air smelt comparatively sweet. It was hotter, unbreathed for a long time and pleasantly untainted by outside influences in the other bedroom. This was furnished much as the one in which the woman slept, except that the bed was single size. The bed was made.

A window which would look out over the yard behind the house was hung with thick drape curtains. The water in the pitcher had a layer of dust over the surface. Aware that he was intruding on the privacy of a stranger, Edge opened one of the bureau drawers and then checked briefly in the wardrobe closet. He discovered the clothing of a man. A tall, lean man. Poor quality clothing, old but well laundered. One suit and fancy white shirt. The rest denim work clothes.

Back in the main room, he had to clean out ashes from the cooking range before he could set and light a fire from kindling and fuel stacked outside the back door. A closet to one side of the range was meagrely stocked with coffee and canned, jarred and dried foods. Water was stored in two drums which stood on another closet next to the larder. In this closet were skillets, saucepans, cups, plates and cutlery. Just enough eating and drinking utensils for two people.

In preparing a meal, the half-breed was careful to use only what he could replace from the supplies in his saddlebags and canteens.

The coffee was ready first and he stood in the doorway, idly surveying the almost barren wilderness in which the homestead was situated as he sipped the scalding hot brew. Behind him, the

11

main room of the house was as spartanly furnished as the two bedrooms with the barest minimum of creature comforts. A pine table with a scrubbed top and a pine chair either side of it at the kitchen end. Two armchairs, a bare-topped sideboard, a table littered with sewing and darning yarns and needles, a bookcase crammed with leather-bound volumes and old mail-order catalogues, a square of rush matting on the floor and two framed prints of biblical scenes on a wall in the parlour area. A kerosene lamp hanging from a hook above the pine table and another standing on a shelf midway between the two armchairs.

All the furniture was store-bought and well made. But old and ill cared for. An overturned empty bottle, an upright but equally empty tumbler and the gentle snoring of the woman in the rancid bedroom explained the neglect. A trail, distinguished from the arid land to either side by the ruts cut by wagon wheels, which led from the front of the house towards the heat-shimmered ridges of the Hatchet Mountains in the south west, perhaps marked the course which the tall, lean man had taken to escape the squalor. Forever or just for a few hours? A husband who no longer shared the marital bed? A son? A hired hand?

Edge drained the cup dry of coffee, got some grounds in his mouth and spat them out into the yard. What did it matter who the missing man was? Likewise, who the woman suffering from sexual frustration and over-indulgence in cheap liquor was. Or why the homestead – well constructed but badly run down – had been sited on this hostile stretch of New Mexico Territory.

He went to the range, poured more coffee in the cup and then ladled some mixed pork and beans from a skillet onto a plate. He sat down at the table to eat, on the chair that allowed him to watch the open front door and the firmly closed door of the woman's bedroom.

She had stopped snoring.

Beth had never snored. During the tragically brief period of their marriage. Working a homestead much like this one. But up in the Dakotas.

His father had. On the farm in Iowa. And Jamie used to say that his elder brother Josiah was a real noisy sleeper.

Edge bared his teeth in a silent snarl and shook his head in self anger. He was not Josiah C. Hedges any more. His father, his kid brother and his wife were all long dead. Like a whole bunch of other people he had known – killed violently or allowed to die peacefully, men and women, good and bad, some killed by the man eating at the pine table in the hot and squalid room and many not, before, during and after the brutal war which had begun the process of changing a farm boy named Hedges into the man called Edge.

He was angry at himself now, as he rattled down his spoon and pushed the empty plate away from him, because he had allowed his mind to reflect on the past. It was a futile mental exercise he had been indulging in far too much recently. At the start there had seemed to be some point to his reflections: there had been a pre-conceived plan to identify the reason why he had become the kind of man he was. Perhaps believing that if he could find the key to this, he might be able to change. Or maybe he had simply sought an excuse – justification for being what he was.

Whichever, it was no longer of any importance. For he had long ago come to accept his lot, if not with deep-down equanimity, at least with stoic indifference.

Then, for a black period, his concern with his past had hovered dangerously close to self-pity as he delved into his memory and elected to dwell only upon those experiences which had robbed him of the people and possessions he held most dear.

Whereas, of late, he considered his penchant for looking backwards resembled the vocal ramblings of old men at bar tables or sitting around grocery store cracker barrels: men for whom the distant years gone by were easier to recall than yester-day and who had neither the faculties nor the energies to fill their tomorrows with anything more than memories.

And Edge was too young for that. But old enough, it seemed – and not sufficiently in control of his own thought processes – for the plaintively sung words of a folk song called *Sioux Indians* to trigger across his mind first one and then many other vivid images of violent incidents from his past.

He had lost Beth to the Sioux.

'Why'd you have to sing that song down here in Apache country, lady?' he asked as he set down his again empty cup,

13

just as the bedroom door creaked open.

'What?' she asked, bleary-eyed, as she took the stopper from a fresh bottle of rye whiskey.

'Nothing,' Edge said with a sigh as he rose from the table. 'Coffee in the pot and some food in the skillet. I can pay you cash for what I've had or replace it in kind.'

'I never eat before sundown, mister.' She leaned a shoulder against the door jamb and tilted the bottle to her full lips, just a mouthful. Then she replaced the stopper. The single snort acted to take some of the slackness out of her stance and put a little animation back in her eyes. 'You're not from around here?'

'I'd guess that not many people are. Except Apaches.'

He glanced out through the open doorway across the broad area of scrubgrass, sagebush and cactus to the heat-hazed Hatchet Mountains in the distance. Cracking his eyes to the merest slits of ice blue against the bright light which now slanted into the room as the sun began its decline down the western dome of the dazzlingly blue sky.

She was struggling to recall something, fastened on it and nodded. 'Yeah, you came in from the north, didn't you? Just before I passed out?'

'You got it.'

'Ain't much life up that way for a lot of miles, that's for sure. Apart from sidewinders and buzzards and a few bobcats. Not even no Injuns, far as I know. But white folks live in San Lucas down on the south-west trail.'

He nodded. As, far out to the south west, the hoofs of a single horse beat at the hard-packed ground. 'Obliged for the information, ma'am. How d'you want paying for the food and coffee? Feed and water for my horse?'

'Name's Lorna Butler, mister.' She was still standing on the threshold between the bedroom and the main room. Continuing to recover by the moment from the effects of drinking herself into unconsciousness. 'You don't owe me nothin', Mr ... ?'

'Edge, Mrs Butler.'

'Call me Lorna.'

'I always pay my way.'

'You already did, Mr Edge. In advance. By bringin' me inside

14

after I passed out. If I'd woke up after sleepin' it off in that midday sun I'd be feelin' a whole lot worse than I do now. And now I feel fine.'

She smiled brightly, as if to prove just how good she felt. The cantering horse was closing with the homestead but she showed no sign that she could hear the steady thud of hooves.

'I'll go along with that,' Edge allowed.

'You could do somethin' that'd make me feel even better, Mr Edge,' Lorna Butler said quickly as the half-breed started for the doorway.

He halted and looked across the room at her. 'What's that, ma'am?'

'Lorna,' she reminded and the brightness of her smile was displaced by seductiveness. 'Won't be right, you callin' me ma'am if you do what I want you to.'

She splayed her legs, placed her hands on her full lips – still clutching the bottle by the neck – and thrust out her breasts.

'No strings, Mr Edge. On account that my need just has to be greater than yours.'

'Obliged, ma'am. But I only stopped by for some food and a little rest.'

'So your luck's changed, hasn't it? Come on over here. I've never been turned down before and no man has ever been disappointed.'

The half-breed was sexually aware of the sensuous woman who flaunted her willing body in the bedroom door. Aware, too, of the rider approaching the homestead: although he was not yet in sight. But the strongest assault on his senses was made by a vivid memory of the filthy and rancid bed upon which he had set down the liquor-sodden woman.

She either saw in his lean, dark, deeply lined face a sign of his arousal or simply assumed that as a man he would be unable to resist the temptation of her wanton offer. And she sought to encourage him by licking her pouting lips and softening her tone.

'Come on to Lorna, honey. You can't tell me you didn't have yourself a little sample of what's on offer when you carried me in here.'

'Company's coming, ma'am.'

She cocked her head, listening. The horse was being walked over the final quarter mile towards the homestead. She was briefly annoyed, then rebuilt the come-hither look across her features.

'That'll just be my boy Cal come home from town, mister. He won't bother us.'

'He'd bother me, lady.'

Her scowl was for Edge now. 'He's just a nineteen-year-old kid, is all. And he don't care what I do, anyway.'

'I care what I do,' Edge answered levelly and restarted for the doorway.

'What's the matter, mister?' she flung after him. 'Don't you have any balls?'

'Yes, ma'am. But I'm particular about the women I ball.'

'Man, did I make a mistake about you, you sonofabitch!'

'Yes, ma'am,' he muttered as he stepped out onto the stoop. 'You were wrong. And I try never to make a mistake.'

He was outside, looking toward the approaching rider, when Lorna Butler hurled the bottle. It hit the door-frame, shattered and sprayed strong-smelling rye whiskey and sun-glinting shards of glass across the stoop.

'Damn, damn, damn, shit!' the woman shrieked as she realised what the outburst of temper had cost her. 'That was my last friggin' bottle!'

'And it's a long time until sundown,' Edge responded softly as he headed along the front of the house and then the side to the yard out back.

The lone rider on the trail was demanding a gallop from his horse now, after having seen the half-breed emerge from the house.

In the stable, Edge took his time at saddling the fed and rested grey mare and encouraging her out from the stall. While he was doing this he heard the rider halt his mount out front of the house and yell: 'Ma, who was that?' as he leapt to the ground. Then less stridently spoken words: from both mother and son as they talked inside the house. Only the sounds of their voices carried out across the yard and into the stable: not the words themselves.

A few moments later, as the half-breed led the mare from the shaded stable into the glaring sun, the rear door of the house was wrenched open.

'Hey, you! What the hell do you think you're doin'?'

Over the distance at which he had last seen Cal Butler galloping his horse ahead of an elongated cloud of grey dust, Edge received a general impression which matched the clothing in the boy's wardrobe. Six feet tall with a rangy build. Now, as the youngster stepped out into the yard, he could be studied in more detail. He had the same hair colour as his mother, but wore it longer than she did: in a similar style to the half-breed. He had also inherited Lorna Butler's good looks, but in a very masculine fashion – the features rough hewn, the green eyes not so large and the jaw aggressive in its thrust. He had been shaving for long enough to have a dark shadowing on his cheeks and jaw although the day was only halfway through its course. He was dressed in patched and shiny work clothes, the black Stetson looking to be the oldest item of his apparel. Around his waist was a gunbelt with the holster worn high, the wooden butt of the ancient Colt Paterson jutting forward for a left-hand cross draw.

His flesh and clothing were sweat-stained and dusty from the ride. Anger, perhaps augmented by fear as he received a close-up view of Edge, caused fresh sweat to dampen his frown-lined forehead.

'Figured on leaving, feller,' the half-breed replied evenly.

'Just like that, uh?' Cal Butler snarled, his rage mounting.

'Son,' his mother whispered anxiously from within the house.

'Good reason I should stay?'

'With six feet of dirt on top of you, you won't be goin' no place, mister!'

He was standing full on to where Edge had halted, the half-breed's left hand holding the reins of the mare. His right hand hung loosely at his side, a few inches away from the Remington butt. Both Butler's thumbs were hooked behind his gunbelt buckle.

'It don't matter, Cal!' Lorna Butler urged.

Edge sighed and nodded. 'You're calling the shots, feller. But listen. If you get that old fiveshooter out of the holster and aimed at me, be sure to kill me. Always try to give folks the warning, if there's time.'

'You give my Ma a bad time!' The fear was showing through the anger now, triggered by the unmoving stance, soft tones and impassive expression of the half-breed. Compounded by his own doubt as he recognised something familiar in his mother's voice.

'By not giving her a good time,' Edge allowed.

'That weren't your idea, way she tells it!'

His youth was against him. An older man, who had learned from the harshness of life that damaged pride was easier to salve than injured flesh would probably have backed down. But Cal Butler felt he had to finish what he started. And he streaked his left hand across in front of his right.

'Crazy kid,' Edge rasped between clenched teeth. And had the Remington drawn, levelled and cocked before Butler had fisted his hand around the butt of the ancient Colt.

'He's all I've got!' Lorna Butler shrieked, hysterical with desperation.

'Freeze!'

Butler ignored the command and jerked the gun awkwardly clear of the holster.

Edge squeezed the Remington's trigger. Fired with the revolver low down, eighteen inches in front of his body. The bullet drilled a neat hole into Butler's left upper arm. And exited through the back amid a spray of crimson droplets. As the injured youngster was spun into a half turn, his own gun flying out of his hand, the blood splashed on the threshold and the damaging bullet cracked across the main room and shattered the already cracked window at the front of the house. Butler's back thudded into the door-frame and he gasped and went down on to his haunches.

'Cal!' his mother shrieked, throwing herself down beside the youngster.

As Edge flipped open the chamber cover, used the ejector rod to push out the expended shellcase and reloaded.

'I'm okay, Ma!' the boy protested, but accepted her help in getting to his feet as Edge, the Remington back in its holster, swung up astride the saddle. He glowered at the half-breed. 'He winged me, is all.'

The glower increased in malevolence as Edge settled in the saddle. This in stark contrast to the expression of ingratiating adulation which his mother directed towards the mounted man.

'You could have killed him, couldn't you? I want to thank you. I want to thank you. It's all been my fault and I don't deserve—'

'Quit it, Ma!' Cal cut in shrilly. 'He's just a cheap gunslinger and we don't have to toady to the likes of him!'

With a choked cry of alarm, the woman stepped in front of her son, fearful that Edge might respond to the taunt with another, more damaging gunshot. She even spread her arms to the sides to emphasise the protective stance.

But the tall, lean man astride the mare simply tugged on the reins and tapped the animal's flank with his heels. To head for the gap between the corners of the barn and the house.

'Thank you!' the woman called. 'I'm really sorry for the trouble I caused!'

'Aw, screw it!' her son spat out vehemently.

Edge showed a wry smile with his mouth as he murmured: 'Trouble is, I didn't.'

Chapter Three

San Lucas was seven or eight miles south west of the Butler home-stead, in the foothills of the Hatchet Mountains. It was not so much a town as a scattering of claims across a rocky slope. With at least one tunnel sunk into the ground on each quarter-acre claim. Every claim also had a home of some kind, variously built of timber, adobe, sheets of metal or even burlap. Here and there a flatbed wagon was parked beside a shack or tent. Well-trodden tracks zig-zagged among the claims over the perhaps two square miles of land which had been staked by the citizens of San Lucas.

The trail from the Butler place cut a direct line from a fold be-tween two hills up the slope to where a row of more substantial structures was built just below the crest. The trail intersected with the short, one-sided street which ran along in front of the buildings and became an open trail again at the south-western end – reaching up to and curving over the top of the hill.

The buildings on the street were all constructed of timber, single-storey with boarding laid directly on the dirt outside to form a sidewalk. At the centre was the longest and deepest build-ing with a faded paint sign on the roof proclaiming: GENERAL STORE – SALOON – HOTEL – LIVERY. To the right of this was the office of the Texas-Arizona-New Mexico Stageline Company. Next to this a house surrounded by a picket fence with a shingle by the gate proclaiming: SHERIFF LEE TEMPLE. On the other side of the building which provided San Lucas citizens with most of their creature comforts was the MINERS BANK and THE SAN LUCAS MINING EQUIPMENT

COMPANY, with their signs done in gold-blocked lettering on their windows.

From the foot of the slope, the settlement looked – even in the bright sunlight of afternoon – grim, disillusioned and unwelcoming. And as the half-breed rode his horse slowly up the grade between the dilapidated shacks and patched tents, the impression of sullen dejection which emanated from San Lucas was strengthened. Here and there, women of various ages and a few old men watched Edge's unhurried progress from the windows, doorways or tent flaps of their crude homes. None called out or made any gesture of greeting and he could sense their total indifference to his presence. The only sounds in the settlement, apart from the measured clop of the mare's hooves, were muffled by distance, rock and earth – coming from deep inside the tunnels. But the thuds of picks and shovels seeking a way into ore-bearing rocks did not reach up to the street: where Edge read the signs which labelled the buildings, then rode across to the largest one and dismounted. The mare was the only horse to be hitched to the rail outside the single doorway of the multi-purpose establishment.

'Howdy, stranger,' a man greeted cheerfully as Edge crossed the threshold, his tone at odds with the forbidding atmosphere which pervaded outside. 'What can I get you?'

He was a short, fat man of about forty-five with a round, red face under a totally bald dome. He stood behind the saloon counter which ran halfway along the rear wall of the place. The store counter, spread with a display of foodstuffs, dry goods and haberdashery items ran down the wall to the left. There was an entertainments platform across the room from this, with most of the intervening floor area set with chair-ringed tables. A thin woman some ten years older than the man, with a pocked face and absolutely straight grey hair, sat on a stool behind the store counter. She looked up from her knitting as Edge entered, tightened her mouthline to show an even more sour expression, then returned to clicking the needles.

'Beer,' the half-breed responded as he reached the bar counter and hooked a booted foot on the rail.

'Be a pleasure, sir.'

He began to draw the brew from a pump.

The glass into which the beer spurted was spotlessly clean. As was the boarded floor, the panelled walls, plastered ceiling, the tables, chairs, counters and display shelves. So, too, the flesh and grey shirts and white aprons of the cheerful bartender and the woman who grimaced as she knitted behind the store counter. But there was a certain tawdriness about the couple and the place they ran – as if they had to make an effort to conceal disenchantment behind a thin veneer of efficiency.

'Be ten cents, sir,' the bartender announced as he set down the glass before Edge.

Close up, the falseness of his attitude could be seen. The smile of his thick lips and yellow teeth had a fixed quality. And the glint in his small, dark eyes seemed to be comprised of a mixture of enmity and greed.

'Can you get a whisky in this glass, feller?'

'Sure can.' The pudgy hand which had been extended for payment turned and wrapped around the glass.

Edge dropped two nickels on the bar top. 'So why didn't you fill it up with beer?'

The fat man was able to abandon his false attitude and he scowled as he replaced the glass under the pump faucet.

'I knowed he was trouble, Cass,' the sour-faced woman growled dully.

'Obliged,' the half-breed said, his tone still even and his lean face impassive as he took the brimming glass and sipped the beer.

'You know every damn thing, Grace!' Cass snapped as he dropped the two coins into a drawer beneath the counter. They hit bare wood rather than rattled on money already taken. 'Truth is, you don't know nothin'.'

He flicked a cloth at a dust mote which was about to settle on the polished bar top. Footfalls sounded on the boardwalk outside. Then a man entered the building.

'Afternoon to you. Just passing through San Lucas, mister?'

'Sure ain't nothin' for no one to stop long for,' Grace muttered.

Edge did not look at the newcomer until the man reached the bar, ten feet to the left. Then saw a man only an inch shorter than himself. Of about the same late thirties age. But thinner. Beanpole thin. With a hollow-cheeked, sunken-eyed face. A thin moustache along his top lip, the same jet black colour as his neatly clipped hair. The deep-set eyes were also black. Dressed in a brown shirt, brown cotton pants and brown boots. A white Stetson hung between his shoulder blades. A .38 Whitney with a lot of fancy scrollwork engraved in the frame and on the cylinder was stuck carelessly into the right pocket of his pants. Much plainer was the five-pointed tin star pinned to the left breast pocket of his shirt.

'Never stay anyplace long, sheriff,' the half-breed told Lee Temple.

'Usual, Lee?' Cass asked eagerly.

'You know it's too early in the day for me, Mr Lutter,' the lawman replied without shifting his steady gaze away from Edge. Then: 'No offence, mister, but I consider it my duty as peace officer here to keep informed about what's happening in San Lucas.'

Edge was used to being viewed with suspicion by strangers – particularly conscientious lawmen who recognised in his deceptively nonchalant bearing and world-weary coldness of eye a deep capacity for violent singlemindedness of purpose should trouble threaten.

'What the hell ever happens in San Lucas since the paydirt near run out and the Apaches hit us?' Grace muttered against the sound of her clicking needles.

'No offence taken, sheriff,' Edge assured.

Temple nodded in acknowledgement and vented a soft sigh of relief. Then, to Lutter: 'I think maybe I'll break my rule and have a belt.'

The bartender took a bottle of tequila and a shot glass off the shelf and set them down in front of Temple. Who filled the glass, put the stopper back in the bottle and pushed it away. He took the drink at a swallow and shuddered.

'I got reason for asking, mister. You come to town from the east? Through the Cedar Mountains?'

'North. From Silver City.'

'Where we should've set up in business,' Grace complained.

Temple showed a frown of disappointment. 'Don't suppose you saw any hostile Indians in the country you crossed?'

'Didn't see another living thing until I reached the Butler place, sheriff.'

23

Grace made a sound of disgust in her scrawny throat. 'Bet there wasn't anythin' hostile about the welcome you got from that Butler woman, mister.'

Temple sighed again. But this time it seemed to be a time-consuming exercise while he subdued an urge to anger. 'I told you before about that kind of talk, Mrs Lutter,' he said softly, gazing at the woman who refused to look up from her knitting. 'You ought to count your blessings and hold your tongue.'

More footfalls hit the boardwalk. Running. The man in a hurry coming out of the office of the mining equipment company and across the front of the bank to the doorway of the Lutters' place.

'Riders comin', Lee!' he yelled in high excitement. 'A whole bunch of them.'

Temple and the Lutters all looked fearfully at the doorway, then suspiciously at Edge as the half-breed finished his beer.

Edge used the back of a hand to wipe foam off his top lip and said to the lawman: 'If they know me, feller, I don't know it yet.'

The Lutters seemed unconvinced of this, but Temple nodded curtly that he was prepared to accept the statement as true. Then, as he turned to head for the doorway, he transferred the Whitney sixgun from his pants pocket to the waistband of his pants. At the belly, with the butt jutting to the right.

Cass Lutter came out from behind the bar and went in Temple's wake. His wife curtailed her knitting but remained on the stool.

'Who knows,' she said to the slower-moving Edge, 'could be our lucky day. Bunch of high spendin' customers!'

She laughed, scornful of her cynical wishful thinking. Edge ignored her and she took up her knitting again.

Out on the boardwalk, shaded from the afternoon sun by the buildings at their back, several people stood peering intently down the slope toward where a group of horsemen were starting up the grade. Temple and Cass Lutter, a slightly built, bespectacled man of about fifty who had called attention to the approach of the riders, a thirty-year old couple in front of the bank, two young men in the doorway of the stageline office and a girl of perhaps twelve or thirteen at the open gate of the arid garden fronting the sheriff's house.

There was distant shouting in the air and people began to

24

emerge from their crude homes and from the tunnels to watch the progress of the newcomers.

Seven men were coming up the slope: four uniformed cavalrymen riding in a column of two with three bare-chested prisoners between the leading and trailing pairs. They were seen to be prisoners from the sagging lengths of rope which linked them together at their necks. Then, as the riders came closer, the men forced by their bonds to ride three abreast were identifiable as Indian braves.

'Francie, get back into the house and at your studies!' Sheriff Temple barked, raising a hand to fist it around the butt of the Whitney.

'Aw, Pa!' the pretty young girl at the gate complained.

'Do it, Francine!' the lawman roared, adding emphasis to her full name. 'Or I'll tan your rump until – '

The girl said something under her breath that was probably an obscenity. But whirled around, her petticoats crackling, and stormed up the walk to the house front door.

'You men get your guns,' Temple rasped glancing to left and right.

Everyone on the street except for the sheriff and the half-breed went back into their premises. When they re-emerged with a shotgun, two rifles and three revolvers, the woman remained inside the bank.

'Looks to me like the army have got the situation well in hand, feller,' Edge murmured.

Then did a double take at the scene on the lower half of the slope and realised he could be wrong. For the prisoners and escorts were no longer alone on the trail. The further they rode up the hill, the more men, women and some children left their claims to converge into a swelling group at their backs. And the soldiers – a captain, lieutenant and two sergeants – became suddenly aware of this. So that their previous composure was replaced by nervousness as they glanced over their shoulders, raked their eyes to left and right and then peered up at the men with guns on the street ahead.

The two officers were in their early forties, one of the non-coms was more than fifty and the other less than thirty. All of them were travel-stained and trail-weary: unshaven for at least two days, sweat run and with a great deal of grey dust clinging to their flesh, their clothing and their horses. The lines of strain and exhaustion seemed to cut deeper into their weathered skin with each passing moment.

In contrast, the trio of Apache braves looked well-rested and untroubled: untouched by what had gone before and not concerned with what lay ahead. Resigned to their fate, whether it be decided by army justice or civilian vigilante action.

They were all in their mid-twenties, dressed only in white cotton pants and moccasins, metal armbands and leather headbands stripped of feathers. No paint on chests or faces.

'Men from Fort Catlow have no authority in San Lucas, mister,' Temple rasped through teeth clenched in a sneer of deep hatred.

'And strangers that try interferin' in San Lucas business with Injuns'll get treated same as if they was Injuns,' Cass Lutter added with equal enmity.

'You like Indians, stranger?' the blond-headed, pot-bellied young man in front of the stageline office called tensely.

Edge was midway through rolling a cigarette. He ran his tongue along the gummed strip before he answered: 'I don't like anybody, feller.'

'Yeah, you look that kind,' Lutter said and, like everyone else on the street, concentrated his attention on the riders as they neared the intersection.

The half-breed struck a match on the door-frame of Cass Lutter's premises and lit the cigarette.

The senior officer, who had a bushy red moustache and a knife scar on his right cheek held up a hand to halt his men and the prisoners at the far side of the street. And squinted his eyes as he raked his gaze over the line of gun-toting civilians on the sidewalk.

'I told you we should have rode around this place, captain!' the older, thinner, more weathered of the two sergeants growled.

'Is anyone in authority here?' the captain demanded as the stockily built, square-faced lieutenant shot a glowering glance at the sergeant.

'Duly elected sheriff is the best we got,' Temple announced, taking a half pace forward, his hand still fisted around the butt of the Whitney in his waistband.

'Captain Costello, Eighth Cavalry from Fort Catlow, sheriff,' the senior officer said and executed a token salute. Then waved his arm to either side: to draw attention to the crescent of people from the claims which arced around behind and on the flanks of the halted horsemen. 'Be obliged if you would disperse this crowd, sir. So that we may secure the prisoners, refresh ourselves and rest until nightfall.'

'Ask you something, captain?' Temple posed.

'Sir?' Costello was anxiously puzzled by the lawman's deceptively calm tone and attitude.

'Say your wife, daughter, best friend or whatever was murdered and you had the killer brought to you with a rope around his neck . . . would you just go on home on the say-so of a stranger?'

'I told you, I told you!' the older non-com said harshly against a background murmur of many voices agreeing with the sheriff's point.

'Shut up, Jaroff!' Costello snapped, not shifting his suddenly hardened gaze away from the angular, moustached face of Lee Temple.

'You recognise these Indians, sir?'

'It was night, captain. They came and they went in less than fifteen minutes. All anyone here saw was that they were Apaches. The killing was indiscriminate. Nobody's going to give much of a damn which Indian killed his particular kin.'

The younger sergeant, who at close quarters looked to be no more than twenty or twenty-one, licked sweat beads off his top lip. As his pale blue eyes swung frantically back and forth in their sockets, searching in vain for a friendly face. When he failed to find one, he steeled himself to combat the threat of panic and spread an expression of grim determination across his features. Which matched the looks on the faces of Jaroff, Costello and the lieutenant.

'Is anybody going to give much of a damn about killing officers and men of the United States Army, sheriff?' the captain countered.

27

'Or facing up to the consequences of such a crime?' the lieutenant added.

'Who'd know, soldier boy?' Cass Lutter taunted through teeth bared in a sneer.

If any of the captive braves understood what was being said or even sensed the dangerous situation which was developing, they showed no sign of it. In addition to being roped together by their necks, they also had their wrists bound behind their backs and their ankles lashed to the stirrups of the Apache saddles on their ponies. They sat rigidly erect, staring directly ahead into a middle distance that held no fear for them.

Captain Costello became as rigid as the Indians. But with shock. He raked his gaze along the line of men on the boardwalk and then stared at Temple. His voice croaked as he said: 'You mean that every man, woman and child in this town would condone the murder of my men and –'

'That shouldn't be necessary!' the sheriff interrupted grimly. 'All you have to do is ride on out of San Lucas and tell your commanding officer at Catlow the truth. That you were outgunned and we forced you to hand over the prisoners to us.'

'And we're ready to face up to the consequences of that, sir,' the slightly built, pale faced, city-suited man in front of the bank added. He had a Winchester rifle held double-handed across the front of his thighs.

The pot-bellied young man out front of the stage line office also had a Winchester, right hand fisted around the frame and the barrel sloped to his shoulder. The older man at his side carried a revolver which he held loosely at his thigh, aimed down at the broad-walk. The bespectacled man in front of the mining equipment office carried a revolver in a similar manner. Lutter carried the double-barrel shotgun diagonally across his chest, both hammers drawn back. Temple continued to grip the butt of the Whitney jutting from his waistband.

The uniformed men had no way of knowing Edge was a neutral and although no one in the crowd to the left and right and behind them showed a weapon, it probably seemed reasonable to assume that some of them were armed. So the officers and sergeants from Fort Catlow were certainly outgunned.

28

'I figure everyone in San Lucas agrees with what Ross Reed just said, captain,' Temple announced and silenced the murmuring voices which had followed the comment by the man in front of the bank. 'And we'd certainly prefer to handle the situation that way. We have no wish to harm you or your men.'

Costello listened grimly to this, then shook his head. 'There can be no deal of that nature, sheriff,' he said, his voice evenly pitched and his bristled, sweating and dirty face looking less weary. 'These hostiles were captured after a skirmish in which six troopers of my patrol were killed. Ten more hostiles escaped, taking with them a wagon laden with stolen rifles. It is important the prisoners be interrogated at Catlow.'

The line of men on the boardwalk exchanged tense glances while the people in the crowd began to murmur again: their tones anxious.

'Lieutenant Hillenbrand,' Costello said.

'Sir?'

'Sergeants Draper and Jaroff?'

'Yes, sir?'

'Captain?'

The three were as grimly determined as Costello. Deep down afraid and still close to exhaustion: but able to draw courage and strength from each other – perhaps even from the mounting tension which seemed to have a palpable presence in the hot afternoon air.

'It is essential that we eat and rest before we head for Catlow. That building there.' He pointed a filthy finger at the saloon and store. 'That appears to have what we require. We will ride to it and dismount. Sergeant Draper will attend to the horses. Hillenbrand, Jaroff and I will release the prisoners from the ankle bonds and take them inside. You will not draw your weapons unless provoked to do so. In that event, your duty is to protect yourselves, each other and the prisoners. Good luck to you. Forward.'

The uniformed men suddenly looked more weary than ever: almost as if the calmly and quietly spoken words of Costello had lulled them to the brink of much-needed sleep. But they responded without hesitation to the order to move. The Apaches, familiar with the routine which had been established over the long ride from their place of capture, touched their heels to the flanks of the ponies as soon as the captain and lieutenant urged their mounts into motion.

Cass Lutter vented a low snarl and swung his shotgun to the aim, pressing the stock against his shoulder. The Winchester and revolver of the men out front of the stage line office also became trained upon the close-knit group of riders slowly crossing the street.

Ross Reed looked nervously towards the sheriff.

'Lee?' the man who ran the mining equipment company called, his voice shrill with tension.

'Easy, men!' Costello urged and all the uniformed riders kept their hands on the reins, away from flapped holsters and the stocks of Springfield carbines jutting from forward-hung boots.

Sunlight glistened on the sweat beads that bubbled on their foreheads and squeezed between the bristles on their jaws and cheeks.

The crowd which had converged onto the trail and followed the prisoners and escorts advanced no further. It seemed that every pair of eyes, except those of the Apaches and the three men aiming guns directed a stare towards the gaunt face of Sheriff Lee Temple.

Edge saw the hollow-cheeked, sunken-eyed face in profile: saw the sweat sheening the skin and the tic that spasmodically moved the bristles at one end of the thin moustache. For stretched seconds in the hot silence that was broken only by the clop of hooves, Temple attempted to outstare just one man – Captain Costello. He failed and squeezed his eyes tight closed.

'Come on, Lee!' the pot-bellied man with a Winchester levelled from his hip urged hoarsely. 'Give the damn order, why don't you!'

Temple's left hand which hung at his side was clenched into a fist as tight as that of his right around the butt of the Whitney.

'No, Pa, you can't!' his daughter shrieked from the house which was set back behind the line of the other buildings on the one-sided street. 'They wouldn't want this!'

Temple vented a groan of despair, snapped open his eyes and saw that Costello and Hillenbrand were within twenty feet of where he stood.

Edge waited until the lawman opened his mouth. Then drew his

Remington before Temple could speak: cocked the hammer and pressed the muzzle into the nape of the man's neck. He was able to do this without moving his feet – was close enough so that his right arm was still bent at the elbow. The half-breed spat the cigarette away from the corner of his mouth to arc it out onto the street.

'No one has to die, sheriff. But if they do, you're first.'

The riders reined to a halt. Frowns of anger showed on several faces in the crowd on the far side of the street. Nothing changed in the stance or expression of Lee Temple as he said, slowly and distinctly:

'As I was about to say, you men put up your guns and let them through.'

As fast as he had drawn and aimed the Remington, Edge pulled it away from the flesh of the lawman and slid it back into the holster, easing the hammer forward.

'Thank God, Lee,' Reed rasped and sagged, leaning his shoulder against the door-frame of his bank.

'Frig that!' Cass Lutter snarled. 'If you ain't got the guts to – '

Like Edge, Temple did not have to shift his feet. He simply swung his left arm – out to the side and iron rigid – and his wrist banged against the undersides of the shotgun's barrels. Whether by accident of the unexpected impact or because the short, fat man had been intent upon squeezing the triggers, both barrels discharged their loads. To send a great spray of leadshot, smoke and a spurt of flame towards the afternoon sky.

Jaroff's horse made to rear at the sound, but the elderly sergeant skilfully got the animal under control.

'I'm obliged to you,' Costello said as he swung down from his mount, and it was impossible to tell whether he was addressing the lawman or the half-breed.

Among the men on the boardwalk and the people in the crowd, unspoken opinion seemed to be about equally divided between the relief Reed had expressed and the anger of disappointment which Lutter showed.

'A fair warning for you, mister,' Lee Temple said, watching the cavalrymen dismount and begin to free the prisoners from their ponies, but directing the words out of the side of his mouth at Edge,

'I intend to kill you for what you just did.'

The crowd broke up into small groups, animated with tense conversation as they returned to their claims. Reed and the bespectacled man who ran the mining equipment store went back into their premises.

'I ain't feelin' any too friendly towards you, Lee!' Lutter snarled.

The man with a revolver had already gone into the stage line office.

'It's over, Mr Rubinger,' Temple told the rifle-toting, blond-haired, pot-bellied man who expressed the same kind of venomous disgust as Lutter.

Rubinger spat into the dust of the street. 'For now?'

'Waiting a little longer won't hurt us, I guess,' the sheriff pointed out.

Edge turned and went back into the Lutters' place. While the Apaches were still being taken off their ponies and Sergeant Draper waited to gather up the reins of all the horses.

'You done good, mister,' Grace Lutter growled grudgingly as she watched the half-breed approach the bar counter. '*If* the sheriff was fixin' to start the slaughter.'

She had put down her knitting while she listened to the tense exchanges outside. Now she slid off the stool and moved around the right angle of the counters to be by the beer pump when Edge hooked a boot heel over the rail.

'Another?'

He nodded and she started to refill his glass.

'Hey, I got the right as owner not to serve no one I don't want to!' her ruddy-faced husband growled as he entered. 'And I don't wanna serve him nor any of these soldier boys who reckon to come in my place.'

'Hold your damn noise and go start a fire in the stove, you stupid man!' Grace rasped at him. 'They're hungry, thirsty and their money is as good as anybody else's.'

Her husband halted midway across the room, bristling with frustrated anger. 'Don't you push me too far, woman!' he snarled.

She glared at him with sneering hatred as she set the brimful glass of beer down in front of the half-breed. And spat out words like they were foul-tasting pebbles. 'There are times when I'd like to push you off the highest ridge in these here mountains, Cass!'

The man's anger swelled into his throat and choked him into a coughing fit.

'Best do like she says, feller,' Edge said as he carried his drink to a table and pulled out a chair. 'That sounds like it would be a real bad fall from Grace.'

Chapter Four

Edge sat at a table near the rear wall of the saloon, his back to the wall so that he was able to watch the doorway and windows.

Costello organised the pushing together of two tables so that he and his men and the Apache prisoners could all sit together: in front of one of the windows.

'We sell liquor, beer, coffee and chili to eat on the premises, gents,' Grace Lutter offered them.

'Seven of the chili, ma'am. Four cups of coffee and three glasses of water. Maybe seconds later.'

The woman went to a door, cracked it open and yelled the order through to the kitchen. Her husband cursed, but did not voice a refusal to supply what was needed. Then she made to return behind the counter, changed her mind and came to the half-breed's table.

'You mind if I join you, son?' she asked.

'If you don't call me son, lady. I'm as old as I look.'

She nodded curtly, pulled out a chair and sat down on his left. And said: 'When I first laid eyes on you, mister, I didn't like you one little bit.'

'It showed.'

Aged between fifty-five and sixty she still showed, in the bone structure of her flaccid, pocked face a suggestion of once being beautiful. But the disease which scarred her and too many years of hard living had brought her close to ugliness. But now, as her eyes – not quite so grey as her straight hair – peered hard into Edge's face, they showed a deep sadness and the sourness went from her mouthline: and it was for a few moments, a pleasant countenance upon which to look.

'Yes, you are older than Frank was,' she allowed with a sigh, and bitterness took command of her features again.

'Son?'

A nod. 'You have no idea about what you've gotten yourself into, have you?'

'Stopped Temple from having a lot of sleepless nights is all, ma'am.'

'None of us sleep nights much as it is,' she replied, then nodded. 'But I know what you mean. If them soldiers was gunned down, Cass and the others would've been able to ease their consciences by recallin' that the sheriff give the order.'

Edge said nothing.

'Be six months ago next Sunday, mister. Night time, like Lee said out there. Middle of the night. Hard to say how many Apaches came. Twenty, thirty, maybe forty. They came in over the crest of the hill behind this place, yellin' and shootin'. Some of them lettin' loose with fire arrows. Lee lost his wife, Betty, son Patrick and his baby daughter Anne. We lost Frank. Seth Reed who run the bank with Ross lived a couple of days, but then he died. Bob Sweeney has to run the mining tool company alone since the Apaches killed his Ma and Pa both. And all over the hill, people were killed or hurt real bad. San Lucas cemetery is just over the ridge behind us. You can count more than a hundred and fifty markers in there now. Were less than sixty – most over people who died old and peaceful – before the night the hostiles hit us.'

Her voice was evenly pitched and low. But with no other sound except for the angry clatter of pans in the kitchen to invade the saloon, Grace Lutter's words could be overheard by the soldiers. Once, as she was speaking, Sergeant Jaroff attempted to point out that he had already related this story to the others. But Lieutenant Hillenbrand scowled the non-com into sullen silence.

'Just for the hell of it?' Edge asked.

The woman had paused and was staring into space – or perhaps into the past. She needed to shake her head to rid her mind's eye of vivid images.

'No, mister. They reckoned they had good reason, to their way

35

of thinkin'. And who are we to argue with the reason. See, this hill where the town is, one time it was an Apache cemetery. A sacred place to them. But if anyone knew about that when the silver lode was found, they sure didn't give much of a damn about it. Any old bones they come across when they was digging for silver they just tossed aside or loaded on the wagons with the rocks to go to the crusher plant up in Silver City.'

'Way I hear it, ma'am,' Costello put in, 'you people were warned by the military of how the Indians felt about this place.'

'Ain't no one gonna deny that,' Grace Lutter admitted with a brief glance towards the soldiers and Apaches. 'But when we were warned people were diggin' out paydirt easy as findin' sand on a beach. And there wasn't but a handful of Apaches around here after the army from Catlow herded them all on to rancherias east of the Cedars.'

'I was at Catlow way back when that happened,' the veteran Jaroff said, and looked pleased that on this occasion he wasn't scowled or scolded back into silence. 'Them Injuns were real mad at what we done to them. Said they'd come back and they have.'

'Grace, come out here and give me a hand with this grub!' Cass Lutter yelled from the kitchen.

The painfully thin woman got to her feet with a grimace, looking as old and ugly as before. 'Folks here nowadays make just about enough to keep alive. Most were fixin' to leave before the Apaches hit us so hard. Still plan on takin' off for country where the livin's easier. But too many need to get back at the Apaches first.'

She shuffled across to the kitchen door and went through. The appetizing aromas of chili and coffee wafted into the saloon.

'What's a stranger like you doing in a place like this, sir?' Captain Costello asked.

Edge finished his beer and dug out the makings of a fresh cigarette. 'Passing through, captain.'

'Real glad you were around awhile ago,' the square-faced, broad shouldered Hillenbrand said as the Lutters came out of the kitchen, carrying laden trays. 'I have my doubts about what would have happened if you hadn't held the gun on the sheriff.'

'If Lee Temple said he was gonna let you through, he'd have let you through, soldier boys,' Cass Lutter growled, slopping chili out of the bowls as he banged the tray down on the table. 'He's a man of his word.'

'And the best man around San Lucas,' Grace added, setting down her tray more gently as her husband ambled across to take up his accustomed position behind the bar counter. 'You goin' to cut the ropes on the Apaches so they can eat, captain?'

The prisoners were only tied by the wrists now, seated alternately with their captors around the pushed-together tables. Their attitudes of calm withdrawal from events around them had not changed.

'We'll eat, then we'll feed them, ma'am,' Costello replied. 'Don't intend to give them the least chance of escape.'

As the soldiers distributed the food, coffee and water amongst themselves and the Indians, Grace Lutter returned to her seat at Edge's table.

'He probably meant what he said to you, mister,' she warned.

'Who?' Edge asked on a stream of tobacco smoke.

'Lee Temple.'

'I've been bearing it in mind.'

She nodded. 'And if he tries it'll cost him his life, I reckon.'

'Lee can take care of himself,' Cass boasted.

'He talks a lot,' the woman growled, with a curt inclination of her head towards her bald-domed husband. 'Like a lot more around here. The rest of them ain't got what it takes to talk much at all. Temple's the only one worth a damn in time of trouble. Reason we elected him peace officer. Hadn't been for him, a lot more folks would've died the night the Apaches come here. But he ain't no quick-draw gunslinger, mister.'

'I said I've been bearing it in mind, lady. I got no reason to do anything about it unless the sheriff makes trouble.'

'Best you people forget your personal differences,' Costello advised. 'Way things are shaping, there's going to be big trouble with the Indians.'

Booted feet sounded on the boardwalk in front of the saloon as the captain spoke. The beanpole thin form of Temple moved in front of the window on the store side of the building and the sheriff came to a halt on the threshold. His Whitney .38 was now in a holster hanging low on the right from a gunbelt fully stocked with shells. The white Stetson was on his head now. There was an expression of strained patience and subdued anger on his gaunt features.

'Are you willing to tell us how great you think the danger is?' he asked.

While the lieutenant and two non-coms looked at the lawman with animosity, Costello merely shrugged.

'I can understand why feelings against the Apaches run high in San Lucas, sheriff. So I don't hold any grudges.' He finished a final spoonful of chili and started to feed the wall-eyed brave seated between himself and Draper. The Indian accepted the food and water stoically, without enjoyment. 'Can only give you the army's considered opinion, though. There's nothing concrete.'

Temple nodded his acceptance of this as he approached the bar counter. Then nodded to Lutter who grudgingly transferred the bottle of tequila and a shot glass from the shelf to the bar top.

'Two months ago,' Costello began as Hillenbrand and Jaroff started to spoon feed the other Apache prisoners, 'three wagonloads of repeating rifles and revolvers were ambushed south of Santa Fe. Army issue weapons, from Department of New Mexico Headquarters scheduled for delivery to Catlow and Forts Craig and Stanton. It was a bunch of Americans and Mexicans who stole the wagons. But we heard the guns were taken to be sold to the Apaches.'

'And the Injuns sure don't want them weapons to practise drill with,' Jaroff growled sourly.

'Obviously,' Costello said, absently giving the sergeant's comment attention it did not deserve. 'Following the hostile attack on San Lucas, the Apaches who had drifted west from the rancherias scattered.'

'That ain't news,' Lutter growled. 'We looked all over for the bastards and never saw not one of them.'

'Just listen, why don't you, Mr Lutter,' Temple said, and poured himself another shot of tequila. Then glanced at Costello. 'They've started to mass again?'

The captain nodded. 'Be more accurate to say, sheriff, that they have been regrouping. In small bands all over the Cedars. To make it hard for army patrols to find them. But easy for them to mass when the word goes out.'

'That the guns have arrived,' Temple rasped.

'Correct, sheriff. And at least one of the stolen wagons is in the area.'

'With the guns spread around among the bastard Injuns by now, after you let it get away from – ' Cass Lutter snarled.

'We didn't have a chance, mister!' Sergeant Draper flared, his pale blue eyes abruptly blazing with anger. 'Some fine men died tryin' and we done friggin' well to capture these braves!'

'I said to just listen!' Temple snapped at Lutter. Then moderated his voice to address Costello: 'They won't tell you anything, you know.'

The captain tried to give his features a determined set, but then weariness and defeat won out. And he shrugged as he rattled the spoon down in the empty bowl. 'We were almost out of rations and water and ammunition. It would have been pointless and perhaps suicidal to try to track the wagon. I consider I took the only practical course open to me.' Now he did manage to get hardness into his eyes and it remained in the stare which he shared out among the civilians in the saloon. 'And I will only accept criticism of my actions from my commanding officer at Fort Catlow.'

'Ignore what Cass says, captain,' Grace Lutter offered. 'It's what everybody else does.'

'Take care, woman!' her husband countered grimly.

'I'm grateful for the information,' Temple said evenly, ignoring the Lutters. 'The people around here will be glad to know they have a chance to take their revenge.'

'Or get slaughtered, mister,' Jaroff pointed out. 'Brand new Spencer repeaters, new Army Model Colts and a whole lot of ammo!'

He whistled through his teeth.

'And you must be aware, sheriff, that the people of San Lucas can expect no protection from the military,' Costello added.

'Not after they refused to heed advice to leave the area,' Hillenbrand augmented.

'And this community will be just one target in an Apache uprising, Mr Temple,' Costello said. 'According to intelligence reports, the hostiles are intent upon raiding every American outpost. Including army forts.'

'White outpost, captain,' Edge said.

'Excuse me?' the senior officer said, puzzled.

'You said American. The Indians were Americans before anybody else, feller.'

'Injun lover,' Cass Lutter muttered vehemently, to end the tense silence which followed the half-breed's comment.

Costello cleared his throat and said: 'Yes, quite so.' Making it plain that he was agreeing with Edge rather than Lutter.

'You said you might want seconds,' Grace offered.

The captain looked at his men, saw each shake his head, and then yawned. 'It would seem we have had enough, ma'am. What we would appreciate is accommodation where we may rest until nightfall. In safety?'

This last he addressed to Temple and his expression added the query.

'You and your prisoners have nothing to fear from the people of this town,' the lawman assured without enthusiasm. 'Though I'm not going to apologise for what happened when you rode in. Feeling was running high, but now the folks here have had time to cool down.'

'I'll show you the way to the rooms,' Grace Lutter said, getting up from the table and shuffling towards a doorway close to the entertainments platform at the end of the saloon.

The soldiers got to their feet and the Apache braves responded without need of an order being given.

Only Cass Lutter watched the exodus, a sneer of contempt on his ruddy-complexioned face. Temple stared down at the brimful glass of tequila, as if he was trying to decide whether or not to drink it. Edge gazed across the room and out of the doorway: across the broad street which was almost entirely in the long shadows thrown by the buildings, to where the air above the slope was smudged with the smoke of many cooking fires.

As Sergeant Draper, the back marker of the prisoners and escorts, went out of the saloon, Temple raised the glass to his lips, tilted his head back and took the liquor at a swallow. It was his third of the day and this time he did not shudder.

'You never said your name, mister?'

'I get by with Edge,' the half-breed supplied. 'But I don't much care whether my grave has a marker on it. If you're better with a gun than I've heard.'

The tall, thin man shook his head, still not looking at Edge. 'Just that everyone should be called by a name. I haven't forgotten what I said out front of this place, but like Costello said, this isn't the time to settle private differences. Way I understand it, you stopped off at the Butler place today?'

'You got that right, feller.'

'Just Lorna Butler there?'

'Hey, Lee!' Lutter exclaimed. 'You think maybe Cal Butler had somethin' to –'

'Shut up, why don't you,' Temple cut in, and ran a hand over his face, as if he were very tired.

'Her son showed up just before I left, feller,' the half-breed answered. 'She said he came from San Lucas.'

Lutter seemed about to blurt out something else, but a scowl from Temple drove him back into silence.

'Calvin Butler hasn't been in San Lucas for months, Edge. And by all accounts he doesn't spend very much time at home with his mother. When you saw him, he didn't say or do anything that might have a bearing on the Indian situation?'

'No, feller,' the half-breed replied as Grace Lutter came back into the saloon and headed across to the pushed-together tables littered with dirty dishes and cups. 'He didn't do much of anything except fall down when I put a bullet in his arm.'

The woman stopped clattering the dishes, and joined her husband and the lawman in staring at Edge.

'What happened?' Temple asked.

'Your jurisdiction go that far?'

Temple frowned his irritation. 'If you'd shot his crazy head off I wouldn't have given a damn. Unless it had something to do with Apache connections.'

Edge dropped his cigarette on the clean floor and stepped on the glowing embers. 'His Ma fell over drunk in the yard. I put her to bed. She didn't like it I didn't join her and she told her boy I tried to.'

Grace Lutter vented a short, harsh, scornful laugh as her eyes glinted triumphantly. Then she looked pointedly across at Temple and injected a tone of blatantly false benevolence into her voice as she said: 'Fancy poor Lorna Butler being that way, sheriff. Well, I'll be blessed.'

Lee Temple thrust a hand into a pants pocket, drew out a silver dollar and slapped it on the bar top. 'I'll drink the change later,' he growled, then spun on his heels and stalked out of the saloon.

The bald-headed man behind the bar counter guffawed his enjoyment of the put-down. 'Ain't often you say the right thing, woman, but you sure came good there,' he congratulated.

His wife ignored the cynical compliment and watched Edge as the half-breed rose from the chair against the wall. There was a glint of admiration in her grey eyes.

'That must really have shaken Lorna Butler, Mr Edge.'

'She seemed real glad I didn't kill her son.'

'I mean you turnin' down that full-blown body she likes to flaunt so much. Ain't many men around here . . .' She glared pointedly at her husband. ' . . . who have been able to walk away from that woman. Until after!'

She spat out the last two words.

'Time she gives a man, he has trouble walkin' after,' Cass Lutter shot back, and guffawed again.

His wife clattered the dirty dishes angrily as Edge stepped out of the saloon and onto the boardwalk. It was early evening and the entire hillside was in shadow from the reddening sun which was almost completely hidden behind the crest. Smoke drifted in an unbroken layer above the scattering of claims and the smells of cooking were strong in the cooling air. Now that he had been told of the Apache raid of six months earlier, the half-breed was able to view the dereliction and sense the strangely forbidding forlornness of San Lucas in a new light. And he could certainly understand the people's strong desire for revenge. For revenge was what had motivated his actions on many occasions in the past.

But he had no sympathy for the dour citizens of the town. Primarily because he had long ago lost the capacity to experience this and most of the other finer human feelings. But even were this not so, San Lucas had brought about its own trouble. Which was none of his business.

'Mr Edge,' Grace Lutter called from the doorway as the half-breed unhitched the reins of the grey mare from the rail.

He swung up astride the saddle. 'Yeah, lady?'

'Be safer if you wait for the soldiers to leave and ride with them. I heard them talkin' when I was showin' them the rooms. Seems the Apaches are comin' in from all directions. If you run into a bunch of them on your own . . . '

She let the sentence hang as she stepped out on to the boardwalk.

Her voice had drawn others from the buildings. Temple, Rubinger and the forty-year-old, effeminate looking man who ran the stage depot with Rubinger. Ross Reed and the bespectacled Bob Sweeney. All of them emerging from the stage line office, to variously survey Edge with dislike, distrust, anxiety and puzzlement.

The half-breed touched the brim of his hat and said: 'Obliged for your concern, Mrs Lutter.'

'But you're a man who goes his own way, no matter what.'

He tugged on the reins to turn the horse along the street towards where it became a trail again to curve over the crest of the hill.

'Good riddance to bad rubbish is what I say,' the pot-bellied Mel Rubinger growled as Edge rode by the stage line office doorway. Then vented a short, harsh laugh. 'At least it saves you the trouble of takin' out the trash, Lee.'

'Another time and another place, Edge,' the sheriff of San Lucas called after the half-breed.

Grace Lutter also raised her voice. 'With what the Apaches have in mind, I reckon that'll be in either heaven or hell!'

Edge glanced back over his shoulder and his teeth gleamed in the twilight as he showed a wry grin on the lower half of his face. And he rasped: 'Depending on whether we go for the climate or the company.'

Chapter Five

Beyond the crest of the hill the trail continued in a south-western direction, dropping down into a long, shallow valley. The sun was gone from the sky now and a low new moon spread a silvery light over a barren landscape of bleached earth and rocks splashed with a thousand stains of dark shadows.

Immediately in back of the settlement of San Lucas, more than a hundred and fifty of these moon shadows were caused by the low mounds and timber markers of the cemetery. The trail bounded one side of the burial ground and the hill crest another. But there was plenty of room, across and down the slope, for new graves. If anyone was left alive to dig them after the Apaches came to reclaim their own hallowed place.

Edge considered the history and destiny of San Lucas only briefly as he skirted the broad area of neatly aligned graves. Then concentrated entirely on searching for signs of danger in those pockets of deep shadow large enough to conceal one man or a whole group of men with killing in mind.

In fact, he used his eyes, his ears and his mysterious sixth sense for danger with a mere minimum of conscious effort. With the same ease as riding the horse. From habit. Having learned during the war and on the many trails he rode since, to expect the worst at every turn. His continued survival depended as much on this constant vigilance as upon his killing skills, because it was his fate to be dogged by circumstances in which living or dying depended upon his readiness to practise the lessons a bloody war had taught him and a brutal peace regularly reiterated. Kill or be killed situations. Some of his own making – like drawing his gun against Lee Temple or riding out alone into country inhabited by hostile Apaches. Many not – the trouble with the Butlers and the accident of chance which caused him to ride into San Lucas at a time when an Indian uprising was threatened.

So, he did not need to consciously clear his mind of reflections upon other things as he rode slowly down the valley, watching and listening and mentally tasting the moon-silvered atmosphere for some dangerous change in its ambience. But he chose to ignore the recent past just as, during the long ride south from Silver City, he had affirmed his decision to disregard all that had gone before.

At the end of the valley the terrain rose in a series of uneven steps toward a pass through the high peaks which formed the southern horizon. Here the trail began to loop and zig-zag: lengthening the climb but reducing the steepness of the grade so that teams could haul stages and heavily laden wagons up to the pass with comparative ease.

The mountainscape was more dangerous here, in terms of the number of escarpments and hollows, hard-packed convolutions of earth and rocky outcrops where a small army could hide: as a single group or in dozens of scattered positions within rifle range of the trail.

Edge bedded down for the night in a hollow some forty feet off the trail, exposed to as many vantage points above as other pockets of unsafe cover he could see below. But he had seen nowhere that was better as he rode the meandering trail toward the pass and it was certainly more secure than any place on the open hillside where San Lucas sprawled.

The mare, well fed and watered at the Butler homestead and rested in San Lucas between periods of easy riding, accepted foreleg hobbles without protest. While Edge attended to the horse and then unfurled his bedroll, he ate two hunks of jerked beef. Then he settled down to sleep, lying on two blankets and covered with one, his saddle under his head and his hat over his face: right hand fisted around the frame of the Winchester which shared the warmth of the bed against the chill of the night air.

He slept.

Until the sound of a booted foot triggered him awake: to

instant awareness of where he was and total recall of the reasons which led to him being there.

'No, don't kill him!' Calvin Butler ordered hoarsely. 'Hold still, Edge!'

The half-breed had only shaken his head – to dislodge the hat from his face. Now he complied with Butler's urgent command – save for swinging his eyes back and forth along the slivered lines of their sockets.

'They'll do like I tell them, if you do what I say!'

The tall and rangy, sandy-haired young man with his left arm in a dark-coloured fabric sling stood on the lip of the hollow fifteen feet away from Edge and directly in front of him. He had his old Colt Paterson in his right hand, waving it from side to side as if to call attention to the men with him. These were Apache braves, in white cotton pants and shifts, leather breechclouts and with eagle feathers in headbands. Five to either side of him, each aiming a Spencer repeater rifle down at the half-breed: stocks to their shoulders and hammers back.

'Shots will warn the horsesoldiers,' Butler said quickly, looking longer and harder at the arcs of threatening braves flanking him.

Edge subdued his urge to self-anger at allowing the intruders to get so close to him before he awoke. The moccasined Apaches were by nature and training silent movers if the occasion called for stealth. And all but the final step taken by the booted Butler had been masked by a constant sound that travelled up the mountain from a considerable distance: a monotonous sound with no high or low notes which his sleeping mind must have accepted as a natural hum made by unseen creatures of the night.

Awake now, coldly aware that his life depended upon the Apache braves obeying Butler's command, Edge recognised the rising volume of sound as that made by a group of cantering horses.

The Indian to the far right of Butler spoke a short burst of words in his own language. Then: 'He come out from beneath blankets. He throw any weapons on ground.'

Butler breathed a sigh of relief. Then had to clear a seemingly tangible lump of fear from his throat. 'You heard Thundercloud, Edge. Do it.'

The half-breed used his right hand to fling off the blankets and sat up. He lifted the Remington from the holster by a thumb and forefinger and left the revolver beside the Winchester as he eased erect. He stood, hatless, his unshadowed face impassive in the moonlight, and with his hands hanging loosely at his sides.

'Shooting too quick for me, feller?' he asked.

'Silence, white eyes!' Thundercloud barked, reasserting his authority over the group. 'Calvin, watch prisoner. Both die if warning given to horsesoldiers.'

Then he issued a terse order in his native tongue and he and the other braves turned and moved away from the rim of the hollow – as silently as they had advanced.

Butler already had his old-fashioned handgun aimed at Edge, and he started down the gentle slope.

'These Apaches scare me a whole lot more than that warning you give me back at the house, mister,' he growled. 'Move over to the side. Away from your guns.'

Edge did so and looked to the left as the sound of hoofbeats rose in volume. But from the bottom of the hollow it was not possible to see over the rim.

'They the Fort Catlow men and the prisoners, feller?'

'That's right,' Butler answered with a nervous quiver in his voice. 'And Thundercloud wasn't just talkin'.'

'I can see that.'

Edge looked over and beyond the head of Cal Butler, to where four of the Apache braves were climbing an easy-to-scale rock face: their white shirts and pants showing clearly against the dark background – until they reached pockets of cover.

'I sure don't want to die and I got no reason to carry a grudge against you.'

Edge shifted his glinting-eyed gaze to the nineteen-year-old youngster. Butler read a question into the impassive expression.

'My mother told me the truth about you. Told me a lot more stuff I didn't know about. I acted like a damn fool and you could've killed me. I got reason to be grateful, Mr Edge.'

A threatening hiss sounded from somewhere between the rim of the hollow and the trail.

'Get down,' Butler rasped, gesturing with the gun and then dropping on to his haunches.

The half-breed also lowered into a squat, his face betraying nothing of the thought processes of his mind as he heard the riders come around the curve and on to the section of trail that ran between the hollow and the rock face on which at least four Apaches were hidden. The horses held to a walk now.

What concerned him was the possibility that Butler might be distracted long enough for him to reach for and use either the Remington or the Winchester. And he decided the odds on this were better than even. Less likely was the chance that he could escape the guns of the braves. He did not even consider an attempt to warn Costello and his men. For they were too close to survive the hail of bullets that would be blasted at them. And, on the other hand, it could be that Thundercloud planned on making them prisoners without bloodshed – at least until he had freed the captive braves and removed them from the danger of being hit in a crossfire.

Butler swung his head, turning his rough-hewn, sweat-beaded face away from Edge to peer up at the rim of the hollow. And the half-breed felt droplets of salt moisture clinging to his bristles as he struggled to subdue an impulse to hurl himself at his guns on the blankets.

The body of riders was now almost level with the hollow and dust motes rose from under the slow-moving hooves to float through the night air.

'I sure will be glad to reach Catlow,' the veteran Jaroff growled with feeling.

'Real creepy out here in the – '

Draper was forced to curtail his comment by a rifle shot.

Somebody screamed and somebody else cursed. This in the part of a second between the first shot and a fusillade that seemed to shake the ground on which Edge and Butler were crouched.

The half-breed's chance had come and been resisted. For Butler's green eyes were fixed upon him again, as was the muzzle of the revolver held in a rock-steady grip.

Horses snorted and forehooves thudded to the ground after

48

rears. Then the duller thumps of unseated riders falling to the trail.

An Apache word of greeting was shrilly voiced. It was answered in high glee. Then a burst of laughter. The braves on the cliff face showed themselves, rifles raised in triumph: began to climb down and then jumped the final few feet.

Butler, then Edge, unfolded to their full heights. Then, complying with a gesture of the younger man's gun, the half-breed moved slowly up the side of the hollow ahead of his captor.

Costello, Hillenbrand, Jaroff and Draper lay among the legs of the now calm horses and ponies. Untidily inert, their faces and uniformed bodies stained by blood: at least two wounds apiece, their flesh assaulted by bullets exploded over a range that guaranteed hits.

The ambushers were on the trail, knives drawn. Some worked at cutting free the former prisoners. Others made well-practised incisions under the hair of the dead cavalrymen and spilled more blood as they wrenched off the scalps. Just one of the prisoners had a wound – a shallow furrow on his naked right shoulder where a bullet had split the skin. And it was he who interrupted the gleeful exchanges to do a double-take at Edge who stood on the rim of the hollow. Then he broke into a renewed burst of excited talk which drew every Apache eye towards the half-breed. In the subdued silvery light of the crescent moon it was difficult to see what kind of emotions the braves were expressing as they listened to fast spoken words.

'It seems like he knows you from someplace, Edge,' Butler hissed fearfully. 'I hope to God you didn't – '

_ 'We had a drink together, in a manner of speaking,' the half-breed replied evenly.

Thundercloud cut in on the slightly wounded man, to issue instructions. Then, while four of the Apaches took off at a run and the others led the animals away from the four scalped corpses, Thundercloud moved closer to where Edge and Butler stood.

He was a handsome brave in his mid-thirties, with a broad forehead and cracked eyes. Wide-shouldered and narrow-waisted. With a half dozen eagle feathers in his headband.

'You!' he said, pointing a long finger at Edge. 'I am told you had hand in stopping killing of prisoners at San Lucas. For this I do as Calvin ask and spare your life. But you our prisoner. You understand?'

'Why do you need a prisoner?' the half-breed countered.

'I do not need prisoner to ask me questions, white eyes. You need answers, you go ask your maker. You know of what I talk?'

To emphasise his meaning, he ran a hand along the barrel of the Spencer rifle. The metal was still sticky with factory-applied oil.

Edge nodded.

Thundercloud matched the gesture. 'Now you saddle your horse and ride with us to war council, white eyes. You Calvin, I charge you with prisoner. Like just now, he cause trouble, you pay same as him.'

This said, he spun on his heels and returned to the group of braves on the trail.

Calvin Butler sighed again and licked beads of sweat off his top lip. 'You're bein' smart, Mr Edge,' he said a little breathlessly. 'Keep it up and maybe we'll both be able to tell our grandchildren about this.'

'I never plan that far ahead, feller,' the half-breed said as he turned his back on the sprawled corpses and started down the slope towards his hobbled horse.

'I got good reason to,' Butler replied, his tone suddenly lighter – almost excited. 'On account I've got a wife three months gone with a child.'

Edge stooped to take the hobble off the mare's forelegs. 'So how come you're mixed up in an Indian uprising, feller? On the wrong side?'

He led the horse across to his unfurled bedroll, as Butler backed away from it, the Remington in the waistband of his pants and the Winchester clutched in his right hand.

'Little Fawn's half-Apache, mister,' the sandy-haired youngster replied, his tone defensive. 'So what's the right and wrong side in this for me is a matter of opinion.'

'Calvin!' Thundercloud yelled. 'You get up here quick with prisoner or we leave you with horsesoldiers! Like horsesoldiers!'

Edge fitted the saddle to the back of the mare and adjusted the cinch. As Butler scowled his resentment of the harsh-spoken order and threat.

'My opinion, feller,' the half-breed murmured, and spat, 'is that we don't need any vote to figure out you're low man on the totem pole.'

Chapter Six

The bullet-shattered, blood-run corpses of the four men from Fort Catlow were left where they had fallen. To begin the putrefying process, the stench of which would attract the coyotes who would gorge their fill. Then, at sun-up, the buzzards would descend, to squabble viciously for whatever meat was left on the bones. After the birds lumbered into the air and became graceful in flight, the flies would swarm in to attack any morsel which the earlier scavengers had overlooked. Finally, the glaring sun would suck the moisture from the bones. And maybe the bleached, dry bones would remain as they were – abandoned for long enough to turn to dust.

It was nature's way and it worked well enough in such remote areas as the Hatchet Mountains. Better, perhaps, than the conventional burial process of the Apaches or the whites as practised in the past and more recently on the hill where San Lucas had been established. At least decay never became far advanced, the flesh of the dead was fought over only by creatures which required it simply for survival, and the deceased were spared the indignity of being attacked by worms.

Edge was allowed to ride without bonds, down from the foothills of the Hatchet Mountains, through the Apache Hills and into the Cedars. Thundercloud was at the head of the column, followed by the three freed prisoners. Then the half-breed with Calvin Butler beside him. Behind the two white men, five braves, a pair of them in charge of the four army horses on lead ropes. The other four Apaches were posted ahead, behind and to either side of the main group: riding as sentries against the possibility of cavalry patrols.

Thus the half-breed – his revolver and rifle lashed to the saddle-horn on an army horse – had no opportunity to extend the token freedom the leader of the Apache band had allowed him.

The group had set off from the scene of the ambush as soon as the designated braves brought the ponies and Butler's black-and-white gelding from the place where they were hidden. Thundercloud setting an unhurried pace to back track over their own sign, on a course that swung at least ten miles south of San Lucas.

'It'll be more than thirty miles and he won't call a halt unless there's trouble,' Butler announced flatly at the outset of the ride.

'And when we get to where we're goin'?' Edge asked.

'Black Bear Bluff, about ten miles south-east of San Lucas. We'll be okay so long as we keep our noses out of their business.'

'Minding my own business is what I usually do, feller.'

Butler nodded. 'Figured that when I saw you camped back by the trail. The beef between the Apaches and the San Lucas folks ain't none of your concern. Just your bad luck you bedded down right where Thundercloud planned to spring the ambush. We couldn't take a chance on your standin' by and watchin' that happen. Then ridin' on out like it was only a mountain lion jumpin' a pronghorn.'

'We, feller? You being married to a half-Apache girl make you one of them?'

Butler had been riding easy in the saddle, expression neutral and tone of voice level. Now he snapped his head around to scowl at Edge and the words rasped between his clenched teeth.

'Do what you usually do, mister! Mind your own business!'

Thundercloud looked back over his shoulder and the trio of men behind him did likewise: if not understanding the words Butler hurled at the half-breed, at least recognising the tone.

'He rides with us only because it is your wish, Calvin,' the leader of the band said pointedly.

The nineteen-year-old, sandy-haired young man was quick to regain his composure. He even managed to raise a smile. 'A slight misunderstandin'. Personal.'

Thundercloud executed a careless shrug of his broad shoulders and he and the other braves faced forward again.

There followed a long period of vocal silence as the column continued its snaking progress through the mountain desert country under the cloudless, star-pricked sky. During which Edge maintained his watch on the broken terrain, despite the fact that he knew the outriding Apache sentries were better placed and more skilful than he was in seeking the first sign of danger. Also, as shod and unshod hooves thudded against the ground and harness creaked, he sensed that Cal Butler was eager to continue the conversation: guessed the sandy-haired youngster was trying to frame a new opening to approach the subject from a different direction.

Eventually, after perhaps a full five minutes had elapsed, he said: 'My Pa used to get along fine with the Mescaleros hereabouts. When he and Ma were the only whites in the area.'

'Way back.'

'Yeah. Before the War Between the States. San Lucas wasn't here then. Only trail was the California and the nearest fort was Fillmore. There were skirmishes between the Mescaleros and the army from time to time. Every now and then a white traveller got killed because he was a damn fool. But Pa went about his business without any trouble.'

'What business was that, feller?'

'Prospectin'. But never on *El Cerro de Muerto*. That's the Mexican name the Indians use for the place where San Lucas is. Where all the silver was, too, which is why Pa never struck it rich.'

'Your Ma doesn't live in a mine.'

'I came along and the way Ma tells it, she made Pa settle down to somethin' with a better future than scratchin' around in rocks for the chance of a big strike.'

'Raising horses one time, it looked like.' He spat to the side. 'In the wrong kind of country.'

Butler nodded glumly. 'But the kind of country Pa couldn't bring himself to leave for a long time. He had enough of a stake to build the place and buy some prime stock. But he only done it to keep Ma sweet. Give her a place where she could raise me. While he went on spendin' most of his time lookin' for a rich lode. Used to go away into the hills for weeks on end, leavin' Ma to do the best she could to breed horseflesh on scrubgrass.'

Edge yawned.

'I borin' you, mister?' Butler asked sharply.

'I'm tired of being awake this time of night, feller. But I ain't going to get any sleep for awhile. So you talk, if you've a need.'

The youngster was silent for a few seconds. Then, very distinctly, said: 'I'm not ashamed of what I've done.'

Edge nodded. 'That's fine. Because I don't have either the vocation or the inclination to be anybody's Father Confessor.'

'Guess you heard how the army got to take the three Apache prisoners?'

'Matter of stolen guns. Rumoured in San Lucas you had something to do with getting them to the Apaches.'

Butler drew in a deep breath and allowed it to whistle softly out through pursed lips. 'And I ain't ashamed of it, like I said. Not just on account of me and Little Fawn being hitched, either.'

'You ride with the bunch that stole the wagons up near Santa Fe?'

An emphatic shake of his head. 'No. The Indians heard that the guns and ammo were for sale and asked me to do the dealin' for them. And I jumped at the chance, mister. Because of the way San Lucas folks murdered my Pa which led my Ma to becomin' what she is.'

'All of them killed him?'

Butler grimaced, unhooked a canteen from his saddlebag and took a long drink. 'I was just a little kid when it happened. But Ma told me about it. Before she took to drinkin' for most of the time.' The lines of the expression deepened into his flesh as he added: 'And much longer before she started goin' with men to pay for the liquor.' He turned to look at Edge again and a frown of intense sadness showed in the silvered moonlight. 'I didn't know nothin' about that until this afternoon. When you'd left the place and Ma just couldn't stop talkin'.'

'Nobody knows everything about anyone, feller,' the half-breed allowed. 'Especially when they don't spend much time together.'

'Yeah, I . . .'

'You already admitted to the mistake. And I guess I like it better here than being back there on the trail with Costello and his men.

55

We're even. You don't have to feel bad about what happened.'

'But you shot me,' Butler countered without rancour. And hurried to explain why he made the point. 'Reckon that puts me ahead of you in somethin'. Really even things up if you listen to me. Don't ask nothin' else.'

'I haven't stopped listening, feller.'

He sighed. 'No, you haven't, have you? Maybe what I mean is you should do more than just listen.'

'You got a wife. Cry on her shoulder.'

Calvin Butler looked ready to vent anger again. But bit back on and then swallowed the emotion and the words he was about to use to express it. And now Edge took a drink of water, to give the youngster time to organise his thoughts.

'It was just as the war started. I was about five or six. A bunch of men came and started to look for silver on *El Cerro de Muerto*. Supporters of the south, aimin' to mine paydirt to buy guns and supplies. Pa warned them off. But they laughed in his face. So he went and fetched some local Indians. There was a fight and Pa took a bullet. A couple of the prospectors died as well. And some braves.

'Little later the Union took control of this whole area and built Fort Catlow. And everythin' went quiet again until the war was over. When the six men who didn't die on *El Cerro de Muerto* came back and started to dig into the hill again. Seems they'd found out enough before Pa fetched the Indians to know there was rich rock in the hill. The word spread and that's how San Lucas came to be what it is.'

'The same six still working claims there?' Edge asked.

'I don't know. I guess so. Even if they are, there's no way of knowin' if any of them or either of the two that the Indians killed fired the bullet that got Pa.' He peered hard at the half-breed. 'But it's the principle, way Ma and me see it. Way Ma tells it, Pa always knew there was a rich lode under the hill. But he took account of how the Apaches felt about that place. Damnit, he died tryin' to keep the whites off it. And Ma and me were left to scratch for a livin' out at the lousy ranch while the men that killed him – or the same kind, anyway – got rich.' He shook his head. 'Well, maybe not rich. There's always been too many of them with a piece of the lode. But they all made a good living for a good lot of years.'

'How long ago did you give up on scratching that living with your mother, feller?' Edge asked.

He looked briefly ashamed. Then: 'A couple of years ago. Ma don't get on with the Apaches. She ain't never said so, but I reckon it's because she blames them for makin' a bargain with Pa about him never goin' on the hill and strikin' it rich. But me, I'm like my Pa and the Apaches know it. I was always welcome at their camps. Spent a lot of time there when I was growin' up. Then, two years ago like I say, I more or less threw in with them. Way over east on the Hermanas Rancheria. I ain't no proper teacher, but I been able to give a lot of the kids the English language and some easy arithmetic.'

'Your Ma said you were on your way back from town this afternoon.'

Sadness showed on his rough-hewn face for a moment. He tried to mask it with an anger he did not feel strongly enough. 'She was drunk or hungover or whatever. But even if she was stone cold sober, I reckon she'd pretend she doesn't know I live with the Indians. Maybe she's even convinced herself that I don't. I only ever call there every three months or so. To see if she's okay and to give her some money. We never talk about what I'm doin'. We never talk much about anythin'. Now that Little Fawn's gonna have a kid, I planned to tell Ma about me bein' married when I went there yesterday. That and to warn her to leave the ranch. At least until the uprisin's over. But in the end, I didn't tell her nothin'. Except called her a stinkin' whore and left to go back to Black Bear Bluff. Afraid I might have killed her if I stayed any longer.'

He sucked at his canteen again. But did not swallow the water. Instead, swilled it around in his mouth and spat it out with the bad taste that had coated his palate.

'Guess her kind of drinking costs more than you can earn teaching at a rancheria school, feller.'

'I know it. Now I know it. You seen the place. First, after I left, she kept runnin' the ranch. Then she started to sell off pieces of the home. Last time I was there, she said she was usin' money Pa left her. But this afternoon she told me there never was any money. So she took up offers that some of the San Lucas miners made her

57

awhile back.' He turned his head sharply away as Edge looked at him, but not before the half-breed saw the glitter of held-back tears at the corners of the green eyes. 'One bottle a tumble, damnit! If there's something blue hangin' on the clothesline, hold back out in the country until you neighbour's through!'

Edge said nothing while Cal Butler used a pretence at blowing his nose to cover the wiping of the teardrops from his eyes.

'Okay,' the youngster went on, as if hurrying to answer a question before Edge had time to ask it. 'I left Ma in the lurch and she had to do somethin' to stay alive and make life worth livin'. So maybe I shouldn't take it so hard. And I wouldn't, if it wasn't San Lucas men she was sellin' herself to. They hate her. Hate her because of how Pa and me get on so well – got on so well – with the Apaches. More than ever after the raid on San Lucas a few months ago. But they use her to make up for whatever they don't get from their wives. And you know what galls me the most, mister?'

'I guess that the feller who killed your Pa could be one of those who visit her,' the half-breed answered.

'Right. That's a pretty poisonous thought to have runnin' around inside your head. When she's your mother.'

'Yeah,' Edge agreed. 'But you didn't know anything about that when you did the gun dealing.'

Thundercloud looked back over his shoulder for the first time in more than half an hour, his face grim set.

'Enough talk, Calvin,' he instructed. 'This white eyes you consider friend claims no interest in the affairs of others. But I think behind mask he too eager to know much.'

'I'm through,' the sandy-haired youngster answered with a sigh. 'But I needed to talk to somebody. I feel better now.'

'Then purpose has been served,' the Apache leader said, and fixed his dark eyes in a long and hard stare at that section of Edge's face not shadowed by the hat brim. 'But you, I suspect, have profited little from the talk.'

'Figure I have to be making a loss as far as the Butler family is concerned,' the half-breed replied and the comment triggered a frown of perplexity across the Apache's face. Edge responded with a wry grin and drawled: 'Just loaned Calvin here my ear. And not so long ago I turned down advances from his Ma.'

Chapter Seven

The morning sun was high and hot when Thundercloud led the band of Apaches and the two white men into the camp under Black Bear Bluff: deep in the Cedar Mountains, at the southern end, close to the territorial border between the United States and Mexico.

An hour earlier and perhaps three miles in a direct line from the camp, the riders had seen a forward sentry rise from cover on the rim of a low-sided canyon and wave in greeting. And two more watching braves showed themselves in a similar manner before the camp was reached. Each of them in a position to have a wide angle view over the mountainscape of jagged rock ridges, dry lakes, pebble-strewn arroyos and infrequent clumps of pinon, juniper, squawbush and other dust-cloaked vegetation. Each, also, in a position to see one another: so that the Apaches massed at the camp could get early warning of the approach of newcomers – whether friend or enemy.

The bluff towered to a height close to a hundred feet and ran for perhaps two miles north to south on the east side of the camp. At its base was an extensive shallow-sided depression enclosed on the other three sides by an arc of wave-shaped hills featured with scrubgrass, brush, clumps of low-growing timber and heaps of boulders.

The wickiups of Apaches meeting in war council were erected in concentric circles on the flat bottom of the depression, with a wide open area at the centre. Between the face of the bluff and the eastern side of the camp was a rope corral holding perhaps a hundred ponies. There were between fifty and sixty wickiups, with a corridor cutting through the rings from the west which led into the area in the middle opposite the largest and most colourfully decorated lodge of the chief.

A layer of dark wood smoke, redolent with the smells of burning and cooking, moved gently in the manner of a quiet ocean in limbo some fifty feet above the pinnacles of the wickiups. In front of the wickiups, close to the fires which were now merely glowing embers and ashes, braves and squaws stood in silent family groups, faces turned to watch the progress of the column on the slope.

'Guess you know Thundercloud is only a sub-chief,' Cal Butler said softly, leaning close to Edge. 'The big noise is Chief Acoti. He'll have to okay you bein' here, but he likes me.'

'You're a useful feller to know in this neck of the woods,' the half-breed replied in the same low tones as his narrowed eyes raked over the camp.

'Here I'm somebody,' the youngster said, pulling erect in his saddle. 'Any place else, nobody.'

There was no sign of the stolen army wagon, but the slitted blue eyes of the half-breed saw that every brave with warrior status had an Army Colt stuck in his weapons belt. And some held a Spencer repeater in the crooks of their arms. The braves were attired in leggings, some bare above the waist and others wearing decorated vests. There were no war bonnets in sight and there was an absence of paint on their faces and bodies. The squaws wore plain dresses.

Thus, the Apaches gathered below Black Bear Bluff did not at first impression on this bright and hot morning suggest that they were massed for a war council. And as the column of riders moved along the corridor towards the open area with the chief's lodge on the far side the atmosphere of peace and happiness was emphasised by the friendly smiles and words exchanged between the freed prisoners and the groups beside the wickiups.

But there were no children in the camp – they would be in a place of safety, cared for by the old who were also noticeably missing. Probably across the conveniently close border in Mexico. Also, there was the recent memory of seeing the carefully posted sentries. And, in the wake of friendliness towards their own kind, the

Indians looked at Edge with curiosity just a thin veneer over latent hatred.

Chief Acoti emerged from the open entrance of his wickiup as all the riders dismounted on the word of command from Thundercloud, Edge taking his cue from Butler.

At close to six feet, the chief was tall for his race. He was more than fifty and the lines of the hard-lived years showed in the flesh of his ruggedly hewn face. Like all the other Apaches camped under Black Bear Bluff, he looked well fed. But he looked less fit than his braves – even flabby under the leggings, shirt and breechclout that he wore. He did not wear a feathered headband, nor a weapons belt. So that at first glance he appeared to be an Apache who had accepted and made the most of life on a well run rancheria. But a closer look revealed aggression in the unblinking stare of his eyes and the thrust of his jaw: the smouldering fires of anger long frustrated, waiting only for a spark to ignite his feelings into brutal belligerence.

He stood, arms akimbo, listening to Thundercloud's report. Then congratulated the sub-chief, his braves and the trio who had been snatched from the army. All this in the guttural native language of the Apaches.

Edge sensed that Calvin Butler was eager to translate what was being said but recognised the youngster felt it politic to remain silent. Until the braves were dismissed and led the horses away to the corral, leaving just Thundercloud and the two whites before Chief Acoti. But even then, the sub-chief spoke before the youngster could utter a sound from his open mouth.

'The white eyes stranger took a hand in stopping the murder of the prisoners by the people who stole *El Cerro de Muerto*. Also, Calvin claims friendship with him.'

'How are you called?' the chief asked in English that was less accented than that of Thundercloud. Not once had he blinked, his eyes like those of a predatory bird.

'Edge,' the half-breed supplied evenly as, on all sides, the normal morning business of the encampment got underway again.

'Why were you in Hatchet Mountains?'

'On my way to someplace else.'

'Where else?'

61

He showed a ghost of a smile that did not touch his slitted eyes. 'Wherever the living's easy.'

'It is easier in white eyes town of San Lucas than in the mountains. There is food, drink and shelter in the town.'

Edge nodded. 'But word was you people planned to hit San Lucas. I happened to pick the wrong part of the mountains to bed down.'

Thundercloud spoke fast in his own tongue. The chief listened without expression until the sub-chief was through.

Then: 'I will accept the confirmation of Thundercloud that it was an accident of chance which has brought you to this place, Edge. I discount the incident at San Lucas since it is likely your concern was for the safety of the horsesoldiers rather than their Apache prisoners. You will remain here, in the lodge of Calvin and Little Fawn. Until I lead my warriors against those who have stolen *El Cerro de Muerto* from our people. Then you may leave to continue your search for earthly paradise. If you attempt to escape from this place before permission is given, you will be given to the squaws to be put to the most painful death.'

Cal Butler made to turn away, less confident than he had been before the chief started to speak.

'Wait!'

The youngster gasped his nervousness.

Acoti maintained his fixed stare upon the impassive, heavily bristled face of Edge. 'Because friend of Apaches Calvin considers you friend, I allow you to remain here. But you are as a fly in the air to me, white eyes. You are either nothing or you are an irritation. When such a creature irritates me, I deal with it. Thus.'

He withdrew his right hand from his chest and directed a hard slap at his left upper arm.

'You understand what I say, Edge?'

The half-breed raked his glinting slivers of eyes to left and right, over the arced lines of wickiups. Then returned his attention to the chief. 'Figure my wings have been clipped,' he drawled. 'And I ain't the crawling kind.'

Acoti beckoned to Thundercloud and both went into the chief's wickiup. Butler sighed, tugged on Edge's shirt sleeve and made a sideways gesture of his head to indicate that they should leave.

'Wow, I was sweatin' some for awhile there,' the youngster rasped. 'Chief Acoti just ain't the same guy I knew over on the Hermanas Rancheria.'

'That's because he ain't the same, feller,' the half-breed responded, noting how the Indians – braves and squaws alike – pointedly avoided looking at the youngster and himself as they moved among the wickiups. 'He's an Apache so he'd consider himself a prisoner while he was living in a place the whites chose for him. Now he's free and he's relishing the taste. Like all these braves are doing. And he's itching to make the whites pay for making him something that wasn't an Apache.'

Butler looked hard at Edge, surprised and briefly nervous again. But there was nothing in the lean face of the half-breed to back up the suspicion of bitterness that sounded in his tone.

'Well, we don't have to worry about it, uh? None of this is any of your business and I've done what I had to pay back the people of San Lucas.'

Edge caught himself just before he started to speak his thoughts aloud and the two completed the walk to a wickiup in the outer ring, close to the corral, in silence.

A squaw was seated in the triangular opening and did not rise and step out into the sunlight until Butler called cheerfully:

'Little Fawn! Meet Mr Edge. He's goin' to be stayin' with us for awhile.'

She looked to be no more than sixteen or seventeen with Apache features, and hair the colour of wheat ready for harvest. It was a strikingly attractive combination and there was an indication that if she achieved womanhood without running to fat, she would be very beautiful. The broadness of her hips and the bulge of her belly beneath the plain and loose-fitting brown cotton dress were obviously due to the child forming in her womb. The mounds of her breasts were merely hinted at: had not yet begun to swell for suckling.

She had no smile for her husband and her bow for each man was pathetically servile.

'You need to eat? There is groundhog meat and hominy. Some mushrooms and cornmeal gravy. You wish me to cook this?'

Her English was even better than that of Chief Acoti and only the clipped sentences revealed it was not her native tongue.

'Yeah, do that, please.'

'Sounds fine, ma'am,' Edge added to Butler's response, as he spotted his mare in the corral, stripped of the saddle and accoutrements. The army mounts were there among the ponies, too. Saddleless.

'We'll wait inside, out of the sun,' Butler suggested, and ushered the half-breed in ahead of him. As Little Fawn went to the fire, to stir the ashes and cause the embers to give up flames.

It was no cooler beneath the matting stretched between poles that formed the wickiup. But the shade was a relief. Blankets were spread on the ground to form bedding. To one side was a heap of cooking and eating utensils with a box of supplies beside it. Close to this was an earthenware pitcher three-quarters filled with water. Drowned insects floated on the surface.

'Food won't take long,' Butler said as Edge stretched out on one side of the blankets and tipped his hat over his face.

'Just resting, feller,' Edge drawled into the inside of his Stetson, as he interlocked the fingers of his hands beneath his head – both thumbs touching that section of the straight razor which protruded from the neck pouch.

'I'll call you,' Butler offered and sat down in the doorway vacated by his wife.

'Obliged.'

Little Fawn re-entered the wickiup just once, to bring what was needed to prepare the meal and after that Edge was left virtually alone while the young couple spoke softly in the Apache tongue: Butler obviously replying to his wife's questions about the newcomer.

The half-breed relaxing on the blankets, easing the aches of the long night ride from his body, had the razor which nobody knew about. The only other weapon close at hand was the ancient Colt Paterson in Calvin Butler's holster. In nearby wickiups there would be braves armed with the stolen Army Colts and Spencer repeating rifles. There was a whole remuda of horses available.

So all I need, Edge thought with a wry smile twisting his lips, is for every Apache within three miles to go to sleep.

Then he abandoned facetious thoughts and attempted to accept his situation with equanimity – by forcing his mind to become a blank. But that proved too much of a strain – to the extent that he felt his muscles grow tense as the skin of his face was pulled into the form of a scowl.

For it was not within him to resign himself to the circumstance which had existed since he looked up out of the hollow in the dead of the mountain night and saw he was a prisoner. And had been denied freedom just as surely ever since, even though the guns had not been aimed at him after he acknowledged his capture.

So he was as Chief Acoti had been on the Hermanas Rancheria – a caged free spirit. But in such a position, he did not possess the same ability as the Apache leader to adopt a whole new personality. The most he could do was to fake resignation for short periods of time. Which was why he was grateful for the opportunity to withdraw into the wickiup and further hide his true feelings under the Stetson.

He was filled with an ice-cold anger that he had been able to confine in the pit of his stomach for a long time. The worst kind of anger, for it had no tangible target. Since leaving Silver City – even before that, since he rode away from the bloodied town of Freedom – he had done his best to stay clear of trouble.

At the Butler place he kept the drunken woman at bay and handed out the Remington's equivalent of a mild slap to the youngster who was ready to kill him. Which was later to pay a big dividend when Cal Butler saved his life.

In San Lucas he drew his gun again: and again it was to prevent violence rather than start it.

And he had left town, having no desire to be mixed up in other people's troubles. Only to be brought, against his will, among the enemy the citizens of San Lucas were preparing to fight.

At least, in town, he had been a free agent.

'Chow up, Mr Edge,' Butler invited.

The half-breed took a few moments to spread the familiar impassive expression across his face before he sat up, put the hat back on top of his head and accepted the heaped plate of food and the spoon which Little Fawn thrust towards him.

He concentrated on eating the good-tasting meat and vegetables, not realising how hungry he was until he swallowed the first

5   65

mouthful. And he welcomed the fact that Butler was in a talkative mood again: for the act of listening to the words helped him to subdue the futile anger he felt for his ruling fate.

'Them army guns that were stolen outside Santa Fe, Mr Edge?'

'Yeah?'

'We only got the one wagonload. And that wasn't bought.'

'Rancheria Indians never get rich,' Edge allowed.

'I set up the deal to buy them from the guys that stole the guns. But Thundercloud rode in with twenty braves. The guys that were sellin' took account of a double-cross. Had all the wagons rigged to blow up if anythin' went wrong. Lucky for us, one of the charges was a dud.'

'Especially lucky for you, maybe?' Edge suggested. 'Though I'd say these Apaches still don't trust you overmuch.'

Butler, who sat on the other side of the blanket bedding from Edge, swallowed a hunk of baked groundhog meat and grimaced. Little Fawn looked up momentarily from her chore of sewing a tear in a shirt sleeve, then quickly bent her head again. There was a look of deep melancholy on her childlike features.

'You noticed that, uh?' the sandy-haired youngster growled. 'Yeah, I was damn sure the guys with the guns trusted me. And when it turned out they didn't, these people have been treatin' me like they think there's a chance I set up Thundercloud and the others to be blown to bits. Chief Acoti give Thundercloud the job of watchin' near every move I make. Reason I was with him and the braves when they hit the army men last night. And he was hid out in the hills when I went to see Ma yesterday.'

His rough-hewn face showed a sudden smile. 'Lucky for you I was in on that ambush.'

'I ain't disputing that, feller,' the half-breed answered flatly.

The smile went as abruptly as it had come: displaced by tense anxiety. 'Ask you to keep that in mind, Mr Edge. On account that if you don't do like the chief told you, won't only be you who'll suffer. I've vouched for you. And the way these people are now, all I've done for them in the past won't count for as much as a heap of chickenshit if –'

'Don't worry about it, feller,' Edge cut in, and scraped the final pieces of food from the plate on to his spoon and shovelled them into his mouth.

Cal Butler vented a sigh of relief, nodded, and showed a broader smile than before. As his wife set aside her sewing, got to her feet and crossed to stoop and reach for the half-breed's empty plate.

'You have had enough, Edge?'

'Right, ma'am,' he replied through clenched teeth. And, as he hit her, rasped: 'Guess you could say I'm real fed up.'

Chapter Eight

Calvin Butler choked on the curse he tried to vent. As the rim of the tin plate impacted with the flesh of Little Fawn's throat: the force of the blow sufficient to shock the girl into unconsciousness and split the skin.

She collapsed like a loosely packed sack of corn dropped from a great height, blood gushing from the lips of the ugly wound.

Edge had been seated cross-legged. But before the girl became still he was on his knees, his right hand poised above the pregnant bulge of her belly – fisted around the handle of the razor, the pointed blade of which rested on the fabric of her dress. But the glittering blue slits of his eyes were directed with menacing intensity at Little Fawn's awesomely shocked husband.

'Be like worrying about if the sun is going to set tonight, feller,' the half-breed rasped. 'Some things just have to be.'

'You bastard!' Calvin squeezed out from his constricted throat, his voice a mere scratch on the hum of activity which sounded from beyond the wickiup entrance.

'You've already got the idea,' Edge said. 'Keep your voice down and your family safe.'

'Safe? She could be dyin' right now. And the child already dead, way you knocked her down.' His throat was clear now, but he continued to speak softly as his shock-dulled eyes shifted from the wound on Little Fawn's neck to the razor above her belly and back again.

'That could be,' the half-breed allowed coldly. 'And the longer she has to lay here like this the bigger the chance of her losing more than just blood, Calvin. So are you going to do what I tell you?'

'You won't get away from here!' The shock was getting less and anger and hatred were building inside him – seen in his expression and heard in his voice.

'Ease the gun out like you were handling an egg and toss it over here, Calvin,' Edge instructed. 'Down where I can reach it without moving. Then turn around and shuffle over here on your butt.'

The youngster licked sweat off his top lip. 'What you gonna do?'

'Break a rule instead of your skull, Calvin.'

'You're crazy.'

'I'm pretty close to it,' the half-breed answered. 'I can either run amok or stay cool, calm and collected. Either way, there's a good chance of me getting killed. But if the choice has to be between being dead or a prisoner of this war-hungry bunch of Apaches, I'll take the bullet.'

Butler squeezed his eyes tight closed, lifted the old revolver from his holster – awkward since he had to use his right hand – and opened his eyes again. Just for a part of a second he debated the possiblility of getting off a shot before the blade of the razor sank through the girl's belly and into her womb. Then tossed the Colt lightly onto the blanket beside Edge's right knee.

'Why didn't you make that choice back in the Hatchet Mountains, mister?' he asked flatly.

'Now the next part, Calvin.'

The youngster turned his back on the half-breed and used the hand of his uninjured arm and his boot heels to propel himself across the blankets.

Edge picked up the time-ravaged handgun with its folding trigger and cylinder chambered for only five .38 shells. 'On account of when there's life there's hope, feller,' he replied. 'But this ain't living.'

He transferred his grip from the butt to the barrel of the gun.

'You ain't breakin' your rule, mister,' Butler said, his voice heavy with despair. 'Acoti will give me to the squaws and it'll be your fault. So you'll be killin' me for aimin' a gun at you twice. Reason I'm doin' what you tell me is so that you got no call to harm Little Fawn any more.'

The sandy-haired youngster sat with his legs splayed, good arm resting across the front of his body, back rigidly straight and neck pressed down between his shoulders in expectation of the blow. Staring directly ahead, out of the doorway at a restricted view of the rear of a neighbouring wickiup beyond the smouldering ashes of the cooking fire.

'You want me to cave in your skull, Calvin?' Edge asked softly. 'Easier way to go than by Apache squaw torture.'

'No!'

'Like I said, Calvin, where there's life there's hope.'

'Come on, get it over with, damn you!'

The half-breed waited for stretched seconds, as Calvin became even tenser. Then injected a despairing tone into his voice to say: 'Forget it, I can't do this to you, feller.'

Butler sighed and his shoulders sagged as he saw the brown-skinned hand pull the razor away from the bulged belly of Little Fawn.

'You done right, mister and – '

Edge cracked the flat of the revolver butt hard against the matting of hair on the back of the youngster's head. And the abruptly unconscious form folded forward and then tipped to the side – away from the girl. Calvin Butler's breathing matched that of Little Fawn in rate and shallowness. The blow had split the skin and the hair began to stain with crimson. But it had done less damage than if the gun butt had assaulted Calvin while he was in a state of mental and physical hypertension.

Edge gripped the revolver by the butt and folded down the trigger, rose into a half-crouch and turned to go to the curve of the wickiup opposite the entrance. He used the razor to cut a three foot long split in the matting, put it back in the neck pouch and pressed an eye to the slit.

The cold anger was gone now – or, at least, was trapped into a tiny hard ball at the pit of his belly. But it was not replaced by remorse or pity or shame for what he had done to the pregnant Little Fawn and her husband who saved his life. Neither satisfaction that the first and easiest part of his plan had been successful. His mind was concerned solely with what he had to do next.

From the slit in the matting he could see the large gathering of horseflesh in the corral with the towering face of Black Bear Bluff beyond. There were no Apaches in sight. He guessed there would be sentries posted on the top of the bluff, but it was not their job to keep watch on the encampment below. From the low murmur of sound among the circles of wickiups he could visualise the squaws preparing the midday meal while the braves rested in the shade of their lodges. Acoti, Thundercloud and the other sub-chiefs perhaps discussing battle strategy in the chief's lodge.

But whatever the Apaches in camp were doing, none of them would have the specific duty of watching the wickiup of the white eyes and his half-white squaw. Not in the broad daylight of noon. Later, maybe, when darkness descended and the war council commenced. Perhaps then the tall, hard-eyed and soft-bodied chief might post guards on the wickiup of Calvin and Little Fawn: to pre-empt a possible escape bid by the white eyes stranger under cover of night while the majority of braves were concerned with matters of war.

Which was why Edge had chosen to make his move now: taking the latest of many calculated risks in the dangerous life his ruling fate forced him to live.

He snaked out through the slit and lay absolutely still for stretched seconds as the nearest group of ponies eyed him with interest. Then, when the animals dipped their heads to tear again at one of the many bales of hay scattered across the corral, he bellied forward – dust clinging to his sweat-tacky palms and floating up to adhere to his bristled face. The sun beat down upon his back and the backs of his legs: and he felt as if it were scorching the skin – like there was no protective layer of shirt and pants fabric between.

He went under the two strands of rope strung taut between lances which took him out of the cover the wickiup had provided. His breathing sounded thunderously loud to his own ears and he could feel the short hairs on the nape of his neck standing erect.

He was already on dust-covered, hard-packed hay and horse-droppings littered ground that sloped up towards the base of the bluff. His objective of the boulder-strewn, broken strip of ground below the towering red face of sandstone was something over a hundred and fifty feet away. And the higher he moved on the gentle slope, the more exposed he would be to a chance glance from any of the Apaches below. If that should happen, an outcry would erupt and he determined he would empty the virtually useless handgun towards the camp – and thus invite a fusillade of shots from the Spencers. Die in the corral rather than make a doomed run for the base of the bluff.

He reached this decision as he inched across the slope on a diagonal line – lengthening the distance to the bluff but aiming for, then gaining, the unreliable cover of a group of a dozen more ponies. He began to move faster then, without wasting any time to check on the many Apaches in a position to be able to see him when he was above the cover of the horses: bellying catty-corn-ered in another direction. Towards a bunch of other animals, one of which was his own mare. If she noticed the man snaking across the ground to get behind her, she was too busy feeding to recognise him.

Sweating tension stretched or compressed time. It seemed to his tortured mind to take an hour to cross the corral: and the next moment it was as if only a few moments had elapsed. Then in brief periods of rational thinking he realised it was something between the two – had to hope he would soon be able to make better time. For the longer it took to get clear of the encampment, the greater the chance of recapture. For when he regained con-sciousness, Cal Butler would surely raise the alarm: hopeful of earning mercy from Chief Acoti.

Edge snaked under the corral ropes and bellied down into a hollow. Rolled over on to his back and closed his eyes against the glare of the sun. He sucked in great lungsful of air and allowed it to whistle out softly through clenched teeth.

The most dangerous ground had been crossed, but he was a long way from freedom. Fear continued to squeeze sweat beads from his pores and tie his muscles in hard knots. Not the fear of dying – it was many years since he had experienced this. But fear of the process of dying. And Apache women were mistresses of the art of giving pain.

He rested for less than half a minute, and then rolled over on to his belly again to begin moving south: intent upon swinging around half the camp in the cover of the hills and back-tracking on the path along which he had been brought there. For he knew where the sentries were positioned in that direction.

From time to time he peered down at the camp. The slow-moving layer of smoke above the depression was thicker now, permeated with fresher smells of cooking food. Squaws sat by the fires, occasionally stirring the contents of the steaming pots. Here and there a lone brave sat at the entrance of his wickiup, watching his woman prepare the meal. Elsewhere, the menfolk stood in small groups, talking. It was a tranquil scene, the single sour note struck by the absence of children.

It was at least thirty minutes since he left the wickiup through the slit in the matting and the half-breed was suddenly aware that he could have killed the young couple. It was a long time for anyone to be unconscious. And the longer they remained so, the worse their chances of recovery.

But he put this line of thinking out of his mind. And it was replaced, unbidden, by a vivid image of the full-bodied Lorna Butler in the tight-fitting shirt and pants. He cursed softly as a bolt of almost painful sexual lust surged through him.

He had reached a point then, where he was able to rise to his feet. And he cursed again at the bulge in the crotch of his pants. But then the sensation was gone, as he looked along a defile and saw an Apache sentry crouched at the far end – a Colt, tomahawk and knife in the right side of his weapons belt and a Spencer rifle resting across his thighs. The brave had his elbows dug into his thighs and his chin cupped in both hands as he stared out at the terrain spread before the end of the defile.

In the cover of some brush, the half-breed took off his boots, tied them together and hung them around his neck. Then, with the Colt Paterson aimed in his left hand and the razor clutched in his right, he took long, silent strides down the narrow defile. Thirty feet, twenty, ten, six. He was holding his own breath and could hear the brave breathing. He fixed his glinting eyes on the single eagle's feather which jutted from the back of the Apache's headband. Except, just for a moment, he lengthened the focus of his eyes and saw another sentry. Four hundred feet in front of this one and maybe fifty feet lower. Standing on a ledge, rifle leaning against a rock, back to the mouth of the defile as he peered towards the most distantly placed sentry.

Then, as the half-breed devoted his full concentration upon the closer brave, the man sneezed.

'Gesundheit,' Edge rasped, and cracked the underside of the gun barrel against the left side of the brave's head.

Then caught hold of the long hair and jerked the unconscious Apache backwards along the defile – out of sight of the brave on the ledge if he should chance to turn around. And, as part of the same smooth action, he slashed the razor across the exposed throat – pulling his hand clear as the arterial blood spurted.

'Did you just catch a cold, feller,' he murmured as he took the Army Colt from the weapons belt and thrust it into his holster.

He wiped the blood off the blade of the razor on the vest of the dead brave and replaced it in the neck pouch. Then pushed Cal Butler's gun into the waistband of his pants and crouched low to claim the fallen Spencer: at the same time as he checked that the brave on the ledge was ignorant of what had occurred.

The ledge was cut into the face of a thirty foot high escarpment, ten feet from the top. The only way to get close to the brave without being exposed to a chance glance for a dangerously long time was to approach him from above. Which involved a circuitous route and a difficult climb.

Another thirty minutes slid into history and there was still no sign or sound to reveal that his escape from the camp under Black Bear Bluff had been discovered. And the half-breed now spent as much time looking backwards as forwards. Aware that Chief Acoti might well reject a hue and cry in favour of a more subtle attempt at recapture.

As he moved on hands and knees towards the lip of the escarpment, Edge could see – over a distance of about a mile – the sentry perched upon the rim of the low canyon. But, because of the way the ground fell away, into the desert valley between the Cedars and the Apache Hills, he was hidden from the brave: as long as he pressed himself close to the ground.

He took off his boots again and left them with the Spencer some twenty feet in from the lip of the escarpment. And he let the two revolvers and the razor be as he bellied forward, picked up a rock of some ten pounds weight and turned over onto his back. Then levered himself along with his heels, carrying the rock on his chest. Only when he was within inches of the lip did he turn over. Then, taking the risk of being seen by the forward sentry, he rose up onto his knees, lifting the rock chest high. Leaned forward.

The sun cast his shadow down across the ledge and into the gully below. The brave saw this and vented an exclamation of alarm: looked up and behind. Reached clawed hands for his leaning rifle.

Edge had misjudged the brave's position by some four feet. So had to throw the heavy rock to the side rather than merely add power to a straight fall.

If the brave, terror etched deep into the flesh of his face, had chosen to duck back rather than place his faith in reclaiming his rifle, the rock might have missed him. But he sought to evade it simply by craning his neck. So that it smashed into the top of his shoulder.

A bone snapped with a dry and sickening sound. The rock dropped to the ledge, bounced and plummeted into the gully. The brave, his mouth gaping but not uttering any sound, teetered on the ledge, flailing an arm and snaking his legs and body rhythmically in an effort to regain his balance.

'This ain't no time for an Apache dance,' the half-breed rasped. As he dropped down prone again, drew the razor from the pouch and reached out to slash with the sun-glinting blade in mid-air. Knowing there was no chance of making contact with the terrified brave over a distance of some six feet.

But the gesture of attack served its purpose. The Indian instinctively leaned away from the razor. And overbalanced to topple off the ledge. He found his voice then, and vented a shrill scream that resounded across the barren terrain: seemingly powerful enough to reach to the ends of the earth. Then the dull thud of the fall's ending cut off the scream. Followed by an irregular slapping noise.

The half-breed held the same position and saw the brave come into view again: that the sound was caused by the limply flapping arms and legs of the Indian as he tumbled over and over down the final few feet of sloping ground into the bottom of the gully. Until this rolling motion was in turn ended, as the lifeless body with a caved-in head became inert beside the chunk of sandstone which had sealed the fate of the Apache brave.

Edge spat out saliva, pushed the razor back in the pouch and spoke through a wry grin: 'Rock and roll goes down better, feller.'

Chapter Nine

Another high-pitched scream shattered the mountain stillness.
From a distance. Too far removed in time and space to be some
trick echo of the Apache's final utterance.

It came from the east – the direction of Black Bear Bluff. And by
reflex action Edge looked towards the unseen source of the sound
as he backed away from the lip of the escarpment and began to put
on his boots.

Then he snapped his head around to peer westward. In response
to a rifle shot. And was in time to see the forward sentry on the
canyon rim throw his arms to the sides and take a few staggering
steps. Then the rifle slipped from the brave's hand. So clear was
the mountain light, the half-breed was able to see one of his feet
kick a rock which cause him to pitch to the ground. Where he lay
still, a dark stain blossoming across the centre of his back.

A second scream from the vicinity of the Apache encampment
under the bluff reverberated through the air.

And Edge snatched up the Spencer. Did not hesitate before
starting back east towards the camp: without waiting to see who
had shot the forward sentry and how many other men were with
him. Only after he was well advanced over his back track did he
consider the possibility that the rifleman at the canyon was alone.
And he immediately dismissed this line of thought from his mind.
But had to struggle harder to keep at bay mental images of the
suffering Calvin Butler was enduring: these conjured up by the
screams which were now sounding with increasing frequency.

It could be no one else venting such strident responses to brutal pain: each scream urging Edge to greater speed and drawing a bitter curse from his cracked-open lips.

The sandy-haired youngster or his half-Apache wife had regained consciousness and raised the alarm. But Chief Acoti and his warriors had bigger fish to fry than a lone white eyes stranger whose only misdeeds were to be in the wrong place at the wrong time and to abuse the trust placed in him. So recapture was not attempted – the Apaches contented themselves by punishing the young Cal Butler who had in good faith vouched for Edge. A cruel exercise which would whet their appetite for the slaughter to come when they attacked San Lucas.

Or was the half-breed underrating the cunning of Acoti? Had he ordered the immediate torture of the youngster in hope that the escaped prisoner would hear the screams and be moved to do exactly what he was doing? Had another circle of sentries been posted to wait and watch, close to the camp, for the escaper to return as a rescuer?

The rifle shot would surely have been heard at Black Bear Bluff. Would it be assumed an Apache sentry had fired it? Or Edge after killing a brave and claiming his rifle? Or the truth – that a third party was involved?

All of this was speculation, racing through his mind much faster than his booted feet were pumping at the ground and the hot afternoon air was being sucked into and expelled from his lungs.

Then he slowed down, his narrowed eyes under their hooded lids which had been constantly searching for signs of an ambush now lighting on landmarks which showed that he was close to the half-circle of low rises which enclosed the encampment on three sides.

For at least two minutes there had been no screams to give him a sound bearing on his position in relation to the camp. He dismissed the explanation that Cal Butler was dead. For in such circumstances as this, the Apaches would not be so merciful.

Bringing his breathing rate under control and setting his booted feet to the ground silently, he moved at a crouch up the slope to the crest of a rise. The Spencer hammer was cocked behind a breech which contained one of the rifle's load of seven bullets. His glinting eyes raked the top of the bluff and the rocky terrain to either side. For sentries would still be posted in those directions.

He came to a halt, stretched out on his belly, and peered down through the dusty foliage of a clump of squawbush onto the familiar scene in the bottom of the depression.

Familiar in terms of the concentric rings of wickiups and the scattered groups of horses in the rope corral with the layer of smoke cloud hanging overhead. But now there was just a small open area at the centre of the encampment. For all the squaws and every brave who was not on guard were gathered there. Most of them in a horseshoe-shaped crowd opposite the chief's lodge, in front of which stood Acoti, Thundercloud and two other sub-chiefs. Between the large and small audiences, a hole had been dug. And close to the heap of displaced dry earth lay Calvin Butler. He was naked and temporarily unconscious from the loss of blood caused by countless knife cuts in the flesh of his body and limbs. His face was not marked.

Edge ran a bare forearm across his eyes to wipe away the beads of sweat that blurred his vision. And saw clearly the response to a one word order which the arms akimbo Chief Acoti spoke.

Two squaws stepped forward, carrying short-handled shovels. And then three more Apache women shuffled out of the crowd – one of them with a blood-stained knife. A squaw stooped to grasp Butler's ankles and another dropped onto her haunches and gripped him under the armpits. The two with shovels prepared to toss in the first dirt as soon as the tortured man was dropped up to his neck in the hole. The fifth woman leaned down to reach with her free hand and the knife for Butler's crotch.

Edge took aim at this one and squeezed the rifle trigger. Just as a squaw in the crowd shrieked an Apache blasphemy.

The .50-calibre bullet burrowed into flesh under the armpit of the woman just as she was about to emasculate Calvin Butler. The range was about three hundred yards and the impact of the lead sent the victim sprawling over the senseless form of the white man and into a heap at the feet of Acoti.

The half-breed pumped the action of the repeater, shifted his aim to the chief and stayed his finger on the trigger. As, in the part of a second before the Apaches vented their shock, he heard the beat of shod hooves. From somewhere in back of him.

Then the chief yelled an order, as he flung his arms to the side. Before whirling to lunge into his wickiup.

Another rifle shot cracked. And dust and rock chippings spattered through the squawbush.

The Apaches broke from the crowd and scattered among the wickiups.

Edge tilted his head and then swept the Spencer towards a fresh target. An Apache skylined, dark against bright blue, on the top of the bluff. He squeezed the trigger and the highly placed sentry staggered back out of sight.

A fusillade of shots pocked into the hill crest close to where the half-breed lay. He saw the tiny splashes of muzzle smoke among the wickiups. Saw also that there were now just two figures on the area at the centre of the encampment. Little Fawn and Calvin Butler. The woman struggling frantically to drag her husband towards the cover of the hole. Then, just as Edge withdrew behind the solid ground of the hill crest, the unconscious and naked youngster dropped down. He didn't see if the half-Apache girl went in after Butler.

For there was a new, much better sight to hold his attention. As, under cover of a constant barrage of repeater rifle fire, thirty or more men reined their sweat-lathered horses to a halt and leapt from the saddles to race up the hill towards the half-breed.

Lee Temple was in the lead. At the head of the group that dispersed to throw themselves down and belly in a line up to points where they could see the Apache encampment spread below.

Most of the men were San Lucas miners. But Mel Rubinger was on the hill, too. And his effeminate partner in the stage line office. The bespectacled Robert Sweeney. All of them with Colt revolvers. Under half with rifles – mostly Winchesters.

'We got the bastards!' Rubinger yelled in high excitement, and was the first of the group to explode a shot down into the depression.

His shot signalled a fusillade of others and the Apaches were surprised into brief panic. On the chief's order they had begun to advance up the slope, convinced there was just a lone white attacking them. Now, as at least a half-dozen of their number fell dead or wounded, they were shocked and confused.

The gaunt-faced, beanpole-thin lawman from San Lucas bellied up beside Edge, saw the Apaches turn and run in compliance with Acoti's order and growled:

'You looking for a place in the history books, mister – starting a war against the hostiles single-handed?'

He triggered a shot from his Winchester towards the fleeing Indians.

'For a guy who claims to mind his own business, you sure do manage to get mixed up in the thick of other folk's.'

'Not from choice, feller.'

They lay, side by side, looking through the squawbush foliage as the men from San Lucas poured a hail of bullets down into the depression. At Apaches who seldom returned the gunfire now – all of them running for the corraled horses. Some kicking at the ashes of cooking fires as they weaved among the wickiups. To send glowing embers spraying across the blankets inside. So that flames leapt and sparks flew, to ignite the tinder-dry matting. And thicker clouds of smoke billowed across the campsite and rose to thicken the layer above.

'Way I read the sign,' Temple answered, holding his fire, 'You should have been dead back where the hostiles hit those poor guys from Catlow.'

'How come a feller who just happened to get elected sheriff of a place like San Lucas can read a sign that well?' Edge asked.

'I was army in the war. Posted to Fort Whipple, north of Prescott, Territory of Arizona. Learned a lot that's stood me in good stead ever since.'

The burning wickiups provided a screen of constantly moving black smoke through which the whites blasted bullets at unseen Apaches mounting their ponies.

'Stage came into town this morning,' Temple went on, weary and bitter. 'With the bodies of Costello and his men aboard. Raised this posse and went out there. Saw that a man on a shod horse rode with the hostiles towards the ambush. That two rode away. And that you were bedded down close to where the army was hit.'

'And figured the worst, uh?'

Temple shrugged his narrow shoulders. 'Looks to me like you'd made some kind of deal to save your skin, mister. Until somebody set up that brave for an easy shot back at the canyon and then we come across another hostile, with his head caved in, in a gorge.'

'Hey, the sonsofbitches are gettin' away, Lee!' Rubinger yelled.

'Go fetch the horses!' the lawman countered as he and Edge continued to gaze down into the depression. And saw the mounted Apaches racing up the southern slope, firing wildly for effect as they crouched low to the backs of their ponies.

Half the San Lucas men lunged to do as Temple ordered while the others maintained the barrage of gunfire.

'It was Cal Butler did the deal for me, feller,' the half-breed supplied.

A nod and a sigh. 'Figured he was on that other shod horse. What then?'

'Life in a wickiup didn't agree with me. Knew they'd give Butler a bad time for letting me get away. But I wasn't far enough away when they started in on him.'

Temple spat forcefully into the bush. 'They kill him?'

'You care, feller?'

'He's one of them. Worse, I guess. Traitor to his own kind. Like for him to be alive with a lot of years of suffering ahead of him.'

'Hey, we gonna go after them, ain't we, Lee?' Mel Rubinger yelled as he and the other men rose. Grabbing the reins of their horses and gazing towards the dust cloud that marked the breakneck progress of the retreating Apaches.

'Sure are,' Temple assured as Sweeney led the lawman's mount across the slope. 'Let's go get them!'

No man from San Lucas had been injured in the exchange of fire with the Indians. And they grinned, laughed and yelled their high excitement as they swung into the saddles. All except for Lee Temple, who held back when he was astride his horse.

'Leave you to see after Butler, mister? If he's not past helping?'

A nod. 'I got him into a hole. Have to try to get him out.'

Temple scowled, then said: 'Forget what I told you after you stuck your gun in my neck. If you hadn't made it so that brave back at the canyon showed himself I guess it would have been us on the run. If we weren't as dead as Costello and the others.'

'That's nice,' Edge muttered as the sheriff jerked on his reins to turn the horse towards the cloud of dust raised by the mounts of the San Lucas men. 'Be able to rest easy in my bedroll now.'

Temple's sunken-eyed and hollow-cheeked face showed a harsher scowl as he looked back over his shoulder at the impassive half-breed. 'You're a hard guy to like, Edge!' he growled.

One brown-skinned hand touched the brim of the Stetson as the other canted the Spencer to a shoulder. 'Nothing worthwhile comes easy, feller.'

The lawman heeled his horse into a gallop and Edge turned and moved around the clump of squawbush to start down to the abandoned camp.

Most of the wickiups had burned fiercely and fast. Were now just heaps of smouldering grey and black ashes from which fragile wisps of smoke rose. More than a dozen and less than a score of blood-run corpses were scattered on the slope and among the destroyed lodges. Braves and squaws alike. There were only eight animals left in the corral, one of them the half-breed's mare. The army horses and a few ponies had bolted from the gunfire and flames and smoke. Enough Apache mounts so that several of the fleeing Indians would be riding double.

As he ambled through the destroyed camp, Edge kept the Spencer hammer back. And he was ready to swing the rifle down from his shoulder and sweep it to aim if any of the sprawled figures proved to be playing possum. But only the half-breed, the horses and the smoke moved.

He saw the blackened remains of his saddle and other gear at the side of a circular patch of ashes which had once been a wickiup. The shells in his Winchester and Remington had exploded with the heat, buckling and ripping apart the frame and cylinder.

When he came to a halt at the side of the hole, so that his shadow fell across it, a swarm of flies rose angrily into the fire and gunsmoke-smelling air. Only half gorged on the congealed blood of Cal Butler's many wounds. The swarm scattered, to suck their fill at the fresher spillage from the more recent injuries of the slaughtered Apaches.

Up on the lip of Black Bear Bluff, a row of buzzards perched and squawked their impatience. The half-breed wondered idly if

83

the ugly birds were the same ones who had earlier in the day been cheated of a feed on the flesh of Costello and Hillenbrand, Jaroff and Draper.

Cal Butler was curled in the foetal position at the bottom of the hole. He was still breathing, each exhalation stirring the dust in front of his parted lips. When the eye Edge could see opened, it was obvious the youngster had been conscious for several minutes.

'Little Fawn?' he asked huskily. 'Is she . . . ?'

'She's not here, feller. Most of the Apaches got away. Temple and a bunch of men from San Lucas are riding after them.'

The eye closed. But not before a tear squeezed out. 'She's my woman. They didn't have time to kill me. They'll kill her. I oughta have let them blast you last night, you bastard!'

'It was your decision,' Edge replied and dropped to his haunches, set aside the rifle and reached a hand down into the hole. 'Here.'

The tear-glazed eye opened and then the youngster showed the other one as he screwed his head around to look full face at the half-breed.

'Go to hell!' he snarled. 'I'd rather die and rot down here than take a favour from crud like you!'

Edge nodded and straightened up. 'Your decision again, feller. But there's upwards of a dozen buzzards waiting on top of the bluff. Be down here soon as I leave, I figure. Or maybe the Apache will give the San Lucas men the slip and double back. Even a chance Temple and the others will give up the chase and come back this way. And they got no reason to help you.'

'Why the frig should you care?' Butler wanted to know bitterly.

Edge turned his head to the side and spat. 'Can understand why I ain't your favourite person. But the way things are right now, I'm all there is between you and some lousy ways to die.'

'You set me up for the worst way, mister! They were going to cut off my balls, stuff them in my mouth and bury me up to my neck! Wait for whatever lives in the ground to smell my blood and come gnaw me to death!'

'It never happened.' Edge touched the brim of his hat as he stooped to retrieve the Spencer. 'Luck to you, feller.'

'Edge!' Butler shrieked as the half-breed made to turn away.

'Do something for you?'

'I can't move a friggin' muscle!'

There were tears in his eyes again. And a deathly pallor to the skin of his face under the tan. His lips trembled. Terror became deeply etched into his flesh. The tears spilled from his eyes and coursed down the lines.

'Please?' he managed to force out just before the sobs filled his throat and caused his blade-tortured body to quiver as if in a high fever. Then, shrilly: 'Help me!'

'No sweat, Calvin,' Edge answered tautly as he tossed aside the rifle and went out full length on the ground. To reach down with both hands and hook them under the youngster's armpits. 'I owe you.'

Butler screamed, louder than when the Apache squaws were using their knives on him, as the act of raising him stretched his skin and triggered new pain from every cut. Then the sound was curtailed as his body refused to accept more punishment and he plunged again into the merciful darkness of unconsciousness.

Edge eased him clear and lowered his head and shoulders gently to the ground. Fresh blood squeezed from most of the reopened cuts on his chest, belly, arms and legs.

'Yeah, Calvin,' the half-breed rasped through teeth revealed by lips curled back in a grimace. 'I owe you. Reason you're in the red.'

Chapter Ten

Edge brought water, rags, some blankets, rope and two sets of rope bridles and reins from an undamaged wickiup on the fringe of the encampment. And spent about ten minutes bathing the shallow knife cuts in Cal Butler's flesh. Then he wrapped the youngster in the blankets and went to fetch his mare and Butler's gelding.

The buzzards continued to watch, silent now, from the top of the bluff, as the half-breed fitted the Apache bridles to the horses.

'No need for that,' the newly awakened youngster said as Edge picked up the coil of rope. 'I can stay up on my own. If you give me a boost to start.'

'Anything you say,' the half-breed allowed, and helped him to his feet.

The blankets slid off him. And he had to steel himself to ask for further assistance.

'Maybe somethin' to cover me, mister?'

Edge said nothing. He used the razor to cut two lengths of rope from the coil and put two slits in a blanket. Then he draped this blanket over Butler's shoulders, with his arms through the slits, fixed another blanket over his head and held them loosely in place with ropes around the youngster's neck and waist. After he had helped the groaning Butler astride the gelding, he was rewarded with a grudging:

'Thanks.'

Then they rode slowly away from the camp and as soon as they were up out of the depression, the buzzards took flight and, after an initial violent beating of their wings, glided down to feed.

'Where are we goin', mister?' Butler asked a few moments later, riding alongside the half-breed on the hoof-marked trail leading westward.

'Home. Your place.'

The youngster nodded. 'I guess I need somewhere to rest up and that's the only place that'll be safe for me around here. What with the Apaches and the whites both out to get me.'

'What I figured, feller.'

'But it's out of your way. Now I'm on the horse, I'll be fine. I see you got my gun in your belt. You give me that, you can take off wherever it is you're headed for.'

'I'll stick with you, Calvin.'

'Why?'

'It's a long way. You've lost a lot of blood. The sun's hot. Maybe you wouldn't make it on your own.'

They were riding into the sun which shafted down at them from its position in the afternoon sky. So that neither the half-breed's brim nor the cowl-like blanket draped over Butler's head shaded their faces. The youngster's pallid features were contorted into a permanent grimace of pain.

'I'll make it, mister,' he rasped. 'I have to make it. So that Ma can patch me up and I can go look for Little Fawn.'

The impassive-faced Edge made no reply. For a long time, they rode in silence. In the gully under the escarpment, the smashed-open head of the Apache brave was black with flies. Butler glanced at the corpse with the same lack of emotion as the half-breed. When the buzzing of the feeding flies was out of earshot, the youngster said:

'If you gave me back my gun and took off, I wouldn't try to take a shot at you.'

'Forget it, Calvin.'

Another period of silence between the two as they rode through the low-sided canyon where, on the rim of the south side, a brave lay dead. Then, as they swung north, veering away from the dust-covered, well-trodden ground, Butler spoke again.

'You done bad by me, mister. But I reckon I done worse by everyone.'

'You paid, feller.'

'I never was one of them. I bet if Little Fawn had been full-blood Apache, they wouldn't have let me marry her. They used me, is all. Even before those two wagons blew and they figured I might have had somethin' to do with it, they never trusted me. Lookin' back, I can see that now. They just strung me along. Because they knew I hated the San Lucas folks the same as they did. They was just waitin' for somethin' like the gun deal to come along. When they would want a white man to fix things for them.'

Edge merely nodded, in acknowledgement that he was listening rather than as a gesture of agreement.

'And, like you say, I've paid. Not just by bein' given to the squaws, I don't mean. The cuts'll heal. But I've lost Little Fawn and my unborn child – maybe forever. It's my fault that Ma's a whore and a drunk. And I ain't got a friend left – white or Apache.'

'That's right, Calvin.'

They were riding due north now, out of the Apache Hills and along the eastern fringe of the desert valley between the Cedar and the Hatchet Mountains. His admission made, but his mind not unburdened by sharing his thoughts with the unresponsive Edge, Calvin Butler gazed directly ahead, the lines of the grimace seeming to cut deeper into his flesh with every yard they covered. While the half-breed, holding the Spencer against his thighs and belly with his elbows, the reins loose in his hands, maintained his habitual surveillance on the arid terrain that spread in every direction.

His narrowed eyes, glinting slivers of ice blue under the hooded lids, searched for something specific. Chief Acoti and his braves and the men from San Lucas were far away: the Indians probably scattered all over the border country to evade whites. To regroup later. Soon, Temple would realise that he and the others had no chance of engaging the enemy in a pitched battle in the mountains. That if such were possible, the Apaches would have fought at Black Bear Bluff. And once he realised this, the logical conclusion to be drawn was that Chief Acoti intended to achieve his original objective, come what may. Regrouped and with the squaws left in a place of safety, the Apaches would ride for *El Cerro de Muerto*. So Temple and his men would have to do likewise.

Thus it was, based upon this line of thinking, that Edge watched for a single rider. Little Fawn, who could well have slipped away from Black Bear Bluff under cover of the smoke and the frantic retreat of the Apaches. Watched as Edge and her husband rode away, then found a discarded rifle, captured a loose pony and moved out on their trail. Burning with hatred for Edge, irrespective of whether or not she considered Calvin to be a prisoner of the half-breed.

But if the young and pregnant squaw was trailing the two riders she stayed well hidden in the foothills of the Cedar Mountains and took no action against Edge. And the sun was well down behind the ridge of the Hatchets, the crescent moon and glittering stars were bright against the sky, and the cool night air was caressing the exposed skin of Butler and the half-breed when a muzzle flash stabbed through the darkness.

A short-lived finger of dazzling yellow, streaking away from the dark bulk of the Butler ranch house.

Edge hurled himself sideways off the mare, using the Spencer in a two-handed grip as a bar to crash into Butler's side. So that the youngster and he toppled to the ground at the same time. Butler's yell of pain and alarm sounded in unison with the crack of the gunshot.

The bullet hit a rock and ricochetted off to the left, some ten feet in front of where the two men lay and the horses veered away to the sides.

'Shit!' Butler rasped. Then tried to raise his voice to yell: 'Ma!'

A second muzzle flash. From the same spot as before – the stoop at the south-west front corner of the house. The bullet burrowing into the head of the gelding and dropping the horse into an inert heap. Fired by a rifle across a range of more than three hundred yards.

Edge cocked the hammer of the Spencer and bellied towards the dead horse, pulling himself along on his elbows.

'No!' the youngster implored and raised himself up on to his own elbows – cupping his hands around his mouth. 'Ma!' he shouted louder now. 'Ma, it's Calvin! Calvin and Edge!'

The half-breed achieved the cover of the carcase. And took aim across the unmoving neck. Drawing a bead on the area of darkness at the corner of the house. But staying his finger on the trigger. Within a fraction of an inch of exploding a shot the instant another muzzle flash stabbed out into the night.

'Cal? Calvin? Am I hearin' right?'

Lorna Butler's voice was shrill with fear and expectation.

'Yeah, Ma! It's me! Don't shoot no more! Look, I'm gonna stand up and show you!'

Calvin did as he promised. He made it up to his knees, fell over and then struggled painfully erect. He held his arms stretched out to the sides. The blanket cowl had slipped off his head.

'And I got Edge with me! You remember Edge! You won't shoot no more, will you, Ma?'

There was movement on the stoop. Then a sound. Not recognisable as the clatter of the discarded rifle on the boarding until Lorna Butler came running out of the moon shadow, arms outstretched towards her son.

He began a staggering run to meet her, moaning at the pain which the violent movements of his limbs triggered.

Edge vented a weary sigh and got to his feet. And by the time he had reached the mare and started to lead her by the reins, the mother and son were locked in an embrace. She sobbing and he speaking fast, soft-toned words.

When he was close enough to understand the words Calvin was speaking – a stream of tearful apologies – while Lorna Butler was countering with distressed demands to know what had happened, Edge made to swing around the couple. But the woman called his name. Then:

'Will you tell me what's been happening, mister? Why Calvin's dressed this way? And what you came – '

'Okay, mister, you can take off now. You done what you figured you had to and I'm safe home with Ma.'

'And just maybe the two of you can live happily ever after, feller,' Edge muttered. 'But it's a little late in the day for me to ride off into the sunset.'

No longer in danger of intruding on private family talk, he led the mare directly past the Butlers and between the house and the barn. Then across the yard and into the stable. After he had tended to the feed and water needs of the horse, he went around to the front of the house. The door was open and the rifle was gone from the stoop. There was no light on inside. He could hear Calvin talking.

'You got nothin' to worry about, Ma. Chief Acoti won't lead a war party on this place. But best you leave the lamp unlit anyway. I ain't exactly good to look at under this blanket.'

Edge banged the barrel of the Spencer on the door-frame.

'Not good to look at? What you talkin' about, boy? You hurt? Those sonofabitchin' Indians harm you?'

'Come in, if you got to,' Calvin called to Edge.

A match scraped and flared as the half-breed crossed the threshold. And Lorna Butler gasped. She was standing by the shelf between the two dilapidated armchairs. Her son was sprawled in one of the chairs, a Winchester rifle on the floor by his bare feet. Outside, as they approached the house, Calvin had apparently been able to hide his injuries from his mother. But now in the light of the match she could see the scabs on his arms, lower legs and on his chest where the blanket gaped.

'Oh, my God!' she shrieked.

She swayed, and dropped the match, which spluttered out.

'I'll take care of it myself!' Calvin rasped.

Edge crossed to the kitchen section of the room and drew a cup of water from one of the drums. A second match was struck and touched to the wick of the kerosene lamp on the shelf.

'I warned you about runnin' with them savages, didn't I warn you!' Lorna Butler groaned. Her voice was still a little high-pitched, but she had herself under better control now. 'I'll light the range fire. Boil some water. You could get infected all over.'

Edge moved out of her way as she bustled into the kitchen area. And she seemed to be unaware of his presence as he sat gratefully on one of the chairs at the pine table, sipping the water from the cup.

He did not realise how near to exhaustion he was until he was seated. And experienced a brief feeling of admiration for the youngster's stamina as he looked across the room and saw Calvin's green eyes staring at him out of a face that was drawn and etched with great suffering in the soft light of the lamp.

'I ain't gonna say it again, mister.'

'What's that?'

'Thanks. Far as I'm concerned, we're even.'

Lorna Butler was kneeling in front of the range, raking out the ashes. 'Why don't you go to your room, Cal,' she urged. 'Soon as I've boiled some water, I'll come see to your cuts. And I'd like for Mr Edge to stay awhile. He can tell me how you got to be in such a state.'

She was stone cold sober. And it was emotional strain rather than liquor which made her pronounce the words slowly and distinctly: as if she felt that to slur just a single syllable might tip her over the brink into hysteria.

'I'm stayin' right where I am, Ma. While he's around. I don't know why he's still here. Or maybe I do.'

He shifted his attention away from Edge to glance at his mother. She was dressed in the same way as yesterday. And as she stooped and moved, pushing paper and kindling into the range, then setting light to it, her full curves pressed against the tight-fitting shirt and pants.

Lorna Butler looked at her son and confirmed from his expression what she thought she had heard in his voice.

'You think that at a time like this I would –'

'Not you, Ma,' Calvin cut in. 'But it could be that he's been havin' second thoughts about what happened yesterday.'

'Have to admit I thought about it the once, feller,' Edge said after he had drained the cup dry, briefly recalling the sight of Lorna Butler sprawled on the ground in a drunken stupor. 'But we all make mistakes.'

'Thanks for nothin',' the woman snapped as she began to fill a pot of water.

'Don't trust him, Ma. He ain't hangin' around here because he likes the friggin' scenery.'

Edge pursed his lips and let his breath whistle out. Then he took the Colt Paterson from under his belt, set it on the table and got to his feet. 'Needed the drink of water and to sit on something that wasn't moving for awhile, is all.' He took a dollar bill from his hip pocket and dropped it on the ancient revolver. 'For what my horse had got through out in the stable.'

The woman whirled around at the range. 'I'm sorry! Don't go!

I don't know what's between Calvin and you. But I know I've got no call to get on my high horse. I deserve any bad mouthin' you give me.'

'Forget it, Ma!' her son said shrilly. 'We don't need him. We don't need no one. I done a lot of thinkin' on the ride from Black Bear Bluff. Soon as I'm able, I'm gonna go try to find Little Fawn. And God willin', I'll find her, Ma. She's gonna have a baby. I didn't tell you that before, did I? You're gonna be a grandmother pretty soon. In a few months. But the kid won't be born around here. I'll find Little Fawn and we'll all clear out of this part of the country. Build a place like this. But on land where we'll have a chance of makin' a real go of things. Where we'll be able to forget all –'

Lorna Butler's face had become ugly with bitterness from the moment her son revealed that Little Fawn was pregnant. And she no longer listened to him after that – was concentrating on finding the words which would express how she felt.

'Just like your rotten father!' she said at length, cutting across his voice and driving him deeper into silence with the intensity of emotion in her staring eyes. 'The both of you runnin' with the stinkin' savages for just one reason and pretendin' it was somethin' else. Him always sayin' it was so the Apaches'd leave him alone to scratch for silver. And now you. Lyin' about tryin' to hit back at San Lucas folks. And the both of you suckin' up to the friggin' savages because you lusted after their women! Couldn't be content with women of your own kind and had –'

'No, Ma!' Calvin shrieked. And tried to rise from the chair. But his limbs had become too stiff and he groaned in agony and fell back. 'Little Fawn and me . . . she's the only one . . . you got it all wrong!'

'Wrong, have I? Your rotten father screwed around at every friggin' Apache camp where all the squaws weren't toothless hags. And you got his blood in your veins. It got him killed in the end. And look at you!' She spat forcefully into the bubbling water in the pot on the range. 'What was your dark-skinned whore doin' while that was happenin'?'

'Shut up, Ma!' Cal shrieked. 'Shut your filthy mouth about my wife! She ain't no whore. I was the first! She ain't like you! She ain't never spread her legs for a bottle of cheap liquor!' He lashed out with a bare foot and kicked the Winchester: managed to trap the scream of pain in his throat but could not prevent a grimace contorting his features as he suffered the effects of the move and the impact. 'All the whiskey gone from San Lucas now? You started sellin' your body for guns instead?'

His mother used the time it took him to vent his anger to bring her own fury under control. And her voice was pitched close to normal when she spoke: raking her eyes from Calvin to Edge – who had moved to the doorway – and back again.

'I was given the rifle. With nothin' asked in return. By Cass Lutter.'

'That penny-pinchin' crud don't give nothin' away,' her son snarled.

The bitter comment from her intransigent son convinced Lorna Butler that only Edge would listen to her with an open mind. And her eyes pleaded for a hearing from the tall, lean half-breed who stood on the threshold.

'Cass was always good to me. Better than all the rest. He rode out this mornin' and told me about the army men bein' killed and Temple headin' up a posse to go after the savages that done it. He wanted me to go to town with him. Said it looked like the Apaches was fixin' to go on the warpath. And if they did they'd kill any whites they could. But I told him I'd rather take my chances out here than suffer the kind of treatment the women of San Lucas would give me. After I told him I didn't have a gun, he left me the rifle. I took them shots at you because I thought you was savages.'

'All you hit was a horse, lady,' the half-breed said. 'It wasn't mine, so no harm done. Far as I'm concerned.'

'You're all friggin' heart, mister!' Calvin growled.

'He brought you back home,' his mother tossed towards the youngster. Then gazed at Edge to urge: 'Please stay. It's the town the Apaches aim to hit. That's for certain. You head for there, you'll be ridin' into trouble. But if you stay here it could be they'll pass us by.'

'I don't figure I scare them that much, lady.'

She shook her head. 'You know what I mean. It's safer here than in town.'

'Safer still a long way from either place,' Edge answered.

The woman squeezed her eyes tight closed, clenched her fists at her sides and sighed. 'Well, I ain't gonna go down on my knees and beg you to stay, mister,' she said quietly.

'That's right, Ma,' her son put in quickly. 'We don't need him. Hey, I just had a thought. Maybe we won't need to go find Little Fawn. What with all the shootin' and runnin' at the bluff, maybe she ducked outta sight. I told her about this place lots of times. She could be headin' this way even now. You fix me up, Ma, and we'll be able to get the hell away soon as she comes. You, me, Little Fawn and the baby she's gonna have.'

Lorna Butler's once beautiful and still handsome face suddenly looked as haggard as that of Calvin's. She licked her slightly pouted lips, like someone who was thirsty. But in her case, not for water.

'All right, son,' she said, defeated. 'And like he said, live happily ever after.'

Calvin's features became youthful again as he grinned – and there was a glint of triumph in his green eyes as he swung his head to look across the lamplit room at Edge. 'Good-bye, mister.'

His mother was dull-eyed when she nodded, and said: 'You're the kind who has to go his own way, ain't you?'

The half-breed showed a cold grin to each of them in turn, flicked the index finger of his left hand against the underside of his hat brim, and answered: 'Never have been one to run with the pack, ma'am. And you don't need a joker for happy families.'

95

Chapter Eleven

Edge reflected briefly on the Butlers as he rode the mare – still bare-backed and controlling her with an Apache rope bridle and reins – down the south-west trail towards San Lucas. And decided that he wished them well.

Calvin, although he favoured his mother in physical appearance, obviously had – as Lorna pointed out – inherited many of his father's characteristics. And the youngster had set out to achieve what he felt very strongly he had to do by siding with the Apaches against the whites. Naively, maybe, in the way he trusted the Indians. But then the son did not have his father's advantages of maturity and experience. And there had been no serious flashpoint between the Apaches and the whites until the silver lode was discovered under *El Cerro de Muerto*.

While Lorna had been a faithful wife and then a dutiful widowed mother through bad times, until it seemed that fate had robbed her of her son just as surely as her husband was taken from her. And in the even harsher times that followed she harmed nobody but herself by selling her body for the liquor that insulated her against the loneliness of her life.

The half-breed rolled a cigarette, struck a match on the Spencer stock and spat to the side before he lit the tobacco. He closed his eyes for the moment when the match flared. So that in the following moment his pupils were just as dilated as before: able to maintain their apparently casual surveillance over the moon-lit terrain.

Yeah, he wished the Butlers well. But doubted if the unseen

96

wounds would heal as quickly as the cuts in Calvin's flesh. Probably would never heal. The mother hated the Apaches too deeply and her son's wife was half-Apache. The son hated his mother for becoming a bottle-a-screw whore and knew he was to blame.

Tonight, the son needed solace and comfort for his hurt. And his condition reawakened the long dormant maternal instincts within her. But despite these circumstances, Lorna Butler was aware of the loneliness Calvin could not assuage and so had desperately wanted Edge to stay at the house. While to Calvin, the half-breed had represented every San Lucas man who had violated his mother's body.

Edge had left, but not as a final payment of the debt he owed the youngster. They had agreed this account was settled. His reason was entirely practical and a matter of total self-interest. He needed to re-equip himself and his horse and get fresh supplies from San Lucas: while the town on *El Cerro de Muerto* still existed.

He put all thoughts of the Butlers out of his mind as he continued to ride the south-west trail. Not entirely content, for he would have preferred to make better speed. But the mare was as weary as he was, so he chose to conserve energy by maintaining an easy pace: and counted on the Apaches taking time to shake off pursuit, regroup and launch their attack.

Suddenly, his eyes ceased their movement along the narrow slits between the lids. And he gazed, without blinking, at a patch of deep moon-shadow between two rock outcrops where the trail rose up from the desert valley to enter the Hatchet Mountains' foothills.

There was something there. He was certain he had seen the blue light of the moon glint on a metallic object. A gun?

Only his eyes, lost in the shadow of his hat brim, showed that he suspected he was not alone. The way he sat the horse appeared as nonchalant as previously. And he continued to move his head from side to side as the mare carried him up the slope – a gentle grade that was totally devoid of cover until the outcrops were reached. A hundred and fifty feet ahead. Then, a few seconds later, timing the action to coincide with a pebble skittering away from under a hoof of the mare, he clicked back the Spencer's hammer: the rifle carried across his thighs and against his belly in the same

7.

manner as when he rode with Calvin Butler from Black Bear Bluff to the family ranch.

Since that momentary glint of light on something shiny, Edge had seen no further physical proof that the dark gap between the outcrops harboured potential danger. But, as he closed with his objective, he sensed watching eyes. And beneath his casual exterior his muscles were tensed and his mind was coldly planning a response should the threat to his survival become a reality.

The more ground he covered, the better his chance. For although the range was getting shorter, so was the distance to the cover of the rocks. And if there was a gun tracking him, the man gripping it was obviously not confident of his ability with it. Or he would have fired earlier. So a lunge from the horse and a fast roll for the rocks might just –

'My husband? Where is Calvin?'

Little Fawn's footfalls were silent. So it was the sound of her voice to which Edge reacted. Releasing the reins and gripping the rifle as she spoke the first word. But then she stepped away from the rock shadow and into the light. Showing herself to be empty-handed. In time for the half-breed to halt his act of hurling himself off the back of the mare.

He pursed his lips and allowed the breath to pass silently between them. 'Lady,' he said softly, 'I sure didn't expect anything as pretty as you to come out from under a rock.'

She was not so attractive as when he had first seen her: her good looks marred most by the ugly line of congealed blood across her throat. There was also a purple bruise on her right temple. In addition to this, her light-coloured hair was in disarray and filthy and her flesh was stained by dirt pasted to the pores by old sweat. He could see more of her flesh than earlier, for the plain dress had a long tear down the front from the neck to below the small mounds of her adolescent breasts.

Around her neck was a leather thong with a metal pendant in the shape of a heart strung on it. And Edge realised it was this piece of jewellery which had caught the moonlight and warned him of somebody waiting between the outcrops.

Little Fawn saw him looking at this ornament, mistook the reason for his interest and clutched the torn dress bodice together across the barely discernible inner slopes of her breasts.

'Please, I am with child,' she implored.

He looked at her face again and saw now the redness of old weeping encircling her eyes: and the tracks which the tears had made through the dirt on her cheeks. She was only a hairsbreadth away from crying again – miserable and afraid.

He tipped his hat onto the back of his head so that she could see the smile he showed. He tried to make it an expression of warmth but he was out of practice. Certainly it did little to relieve her feelings.

'You've got me wrong, Little Fawn,' he said softly and made to dismount.

But the girl gasped and drew back, half into the shadows again. Edge remained astride the mare.

'This is the trail to San Lucas.'

She nodded. 'I have been there. Close to there.'

'On foot?'

Another nod. 'When the camp attacked, I try to hide my husband. I think no one see this. But Thundercloud, he see me. When people leave to run from attackers, Thundercloud pick me up and put me on his pony. For a long time we run, but pony not go so fast with two. And Thundercloud throw me to ground.'

She raised a hand and touched her fingers to the swelling on her head. 'I fall hard. But able to roll into brush and see the white men ride by before I lose my senses. When I awake, much time has gone. I run back to camp. My husband is not in hole where I hid him. See sign that two men on shod horses have left camp. To west. Sign very confused. But I think Calvin must be taken to San Lucas. But then no sign. Except to south. I go to look at town anyway. No way to tell if Calvin there.'

She came out into the full moonlight again and tilted her head back: as if to ensure that Edge saw the full extent of her desperate misery.

'The baby all right?' he asked.

She looked down at her slightly swollen belly, then explored the contour with both hands. 'I do not know. Only that there has been no pain here. Nor other signs of . . . '

She turned her head away, embarrassed.

'Calvin's no worse than when you put him down the hole.'

Her head snapped around again and her eyes stared fixedly at him for stretched seconds. It was obvious she was unsure of whether or not to believe him.

'Please? Mother of my husband can enter San Lucas. If people there see me, they will kill me. I go to ask Mrs Butler if she will —'

'He's with her at the house, Little Fawn.'

The girl squeezed her weary, tear-ravaged eyes tight closed and moved her lips in a silent prayer. It was impossible to see if she was giving thanks to the white eyes' God or some Apache deity. For a moment after her lips ceased to move, they remained parted to show her teeth in an exhausted smile. Then:

'You, Edge? You took him to home of mother?'

'Yeah.'

'And he will . . . ?'

'Calvin'll heal, ma'am. He's hoping you'll go to him. If you don't, he figures to come looking for you.'

Relief seemed to be acting to drain her final reserves of energy. She swayed, but managed to shuffle sideways and lean her slim shoulder against one of the outcrops which kept her to her feet.

'I must rest. Then I will go to him.' Ever since she had dropped both hands to touch the flesh encasing her forming child, the torn dress bodice gaped. And the half-breed had to make a conscious effort to look at her face and quell the beginnings of sexual desire that threatened to surge up from the base of his belly. 'He is all I have. Until Calvin, I had nothing. Neither from Apaches nor whites.'

'You can have a horse, Little Fawn,' Edge offered. And immediately regretted the words.

But the girl sagging against the rock shook her head. 'No, Edge. Until now I thought I again had nothing. Just hope. You have given me what I hoped for. I can take nothing more from you.'

He glanced back over his shoulder — out along the trail at the end of which was the Butler place. 'I guess Calvin won't be going anywhere for awhile. So you got plenty of time. If Chief Acoti and his braves —'

'The Apaches want revenge only against people who stole the hill of dead, Edge. They made my husband suffer much already.

Think I am no more. Just the white people of San Lucas.' Now she looked back over her shoulder, into the moon-shadow. 'And they will be much pleased if you are there.'

Edge smiled and set the hat back on top of his head, tilted slightly forward. 'Obliged to you for your concern, Little Fawn.'

'But you know this. You are kind who does what he thinks he must – whatever happen.'

'What I must, sure. But not always what I like. I don't enjoy hurting women.'

Now she touched the dried crusting of blood on her throat. 'Like Calvin, I will heal. Take longer to go than the hate I carried for you all through the day and into this night.'

She smiled and did not have to make any effort to inject warmth into her wearily haggard face.

Edge heeled the mare forward and as he rode between the outcrops he said: 'Have a healthy baby, Little Fawn.'

'If it is so, I will remember your wish for it, Edge,' the girl called after him.

The half-breed spoke so that his words reached only his own ears. 'Make a change for me to be well remembered.'

The night was not much older when he rode the mare through the fold in the hills to the south-east of San Lucas and started up the slope of *El Cerro de Muerto*. But the first hour of the new day was almost over and just a single light shone in the darkness. From a window in the house of Sheriff Lee Temple at the far end of the street under the brow of the hill.

As he covered the final stretch of trail which cut between the claims, the only sound was made by the weary clop of the horse's hooves against the hard-packed dirt. He sensed the presence of people in the shacks and tents built close to the mine tunnels, but was not conscious of any eyes watching his progress. Until he drew close to the intersection of trail with street. And saw a human form silhouetted in the light which cut a square in the dark façade of the house. The slight form of a girl. The lawman's young daughter Francine who, with her plea of *They wouldn't want this*, had probably done more than Edge's threatening gun to give the four cavalrymen a few more hours of life.

Who had she meant by *they*? Not the living. Most of the citizens of San Lucas had been ready and willing to see the soldiers gunned down if that was the only way to kill the Apache prisoners. So the dead. Her mother, brother and sister? Or everyone who had perished the last time the Apaches had punished the whites for stealing *El Cerro de Muerto*?

It didn't matter. It was just a line of thought to keep him awake as he completed his long round trip to San Lucas.

As he slid from the back of the mare and began to lead her across the street, Francine Temple withdrew from the window, and let the net curtain fall back into place.

Instead of going towards the door of the Lutter place, he angled for the corner where, yesterday, he had seen Sergeant Draper lead the army horses and Indian ponies on the way to the livery. But he halted when the door creaked open and a booted foot was set down on the boardwalk outside.

'Drop that rifle, mister!' Cass Lutter ordered. 'Or we'll have to shovel you up off the street and into your box!'

The short, rotund man with the ruddy face under a bald head took another forward step and thrust out the double barrel shotgun to the full extent of his reach. The same move allowed his emaciated wife to step across the threshold. She was as grim-faced as he, but her tone was not so harsh when she urged:

'Best do like he tells you, Edge. There are times when Cass means just what he says. And this is one of them times.'

Edge unfisted his hand from around the Spencer before she was half-finished.

'Now step away from the horse and unbuckle the gunbelt,' her husband ordered in the same tone as before.

Along the street, a door opened and light footfalls sounded. Both the Lutters looked in that direction. And Edge knew he had time to move a hand from the belt buckle to the holstered Colt, draw the revolver and put a bullet into the man with the shotgun. But he didn't.

'Why are you doing this?' Francine Temple called shrilly.

'Go back inside, girl!' Mrs Lutter shouted and the sheriff's daughter came to a halt at the gate in the picket fence.

As light spilled from the window of the bank, the door beside it opened and Ross and Susan Reed showed themselves on the threshold. Unlike the Lutters and the Temple girl who were fully dressed, the slightly built, pallid-faced banker and his red-haired, homely wife were in their night clothes. They looked as frightened and confused as the sheriff's daughter.

The half-breed's gunbelt fell in a half-circle around the back and sides of his tall frame. 'The kid beat me to the question, feller,' he drawled.

'Ross, go get his horse and take it round back to the stable! Don't get between him and this here shotgun!'

'Dear, you've got no clothes on!' the banker's wife wailed.

'The hell with that, Mrs Ross!' Cass Lutter snarled. 'This ain't no time to stand on ceremony!'

Edge made it easier for the night-shirted banker. He moved around in front of the mare. Was tracked by the twin muzzles of the gun in Lutter's rock-steady grip.

Reed shot a hard look at Edge as he took hold of the reins, but did not speak until he had led the horse several feet towards the opening between his bank and Lutter's place. Then:

'Hey, Cass! You know what – '

'Yeah, Ross. I seen he was ridin' bareback with Apache tack. He sure has got some explainin' to do. Unless he wants to get his head blowed off his shoulders. Grace! Go inside and light a lamp. And you, mister, you come on in. Real slow and easy. Cause if you make one wrong move – ' He parted his lips in a vicious grin. ' – boom. You know what I mean?'

'That's the third time you said it, feller. And I don't aim to lose my head.'

Light spilled out from the doorway behind Lutter and the windows to either side of him.

'If my Dad were here, he wouldn't – ' Francine Temple started.

'Be quiet, girl!' Lutter snapped and this time did not look towards her. 'Someone has to take care of things when your Pa ain't around.'

He took a short backward step and made just a fractional movement with the shotgun to gesture for Edge to move forward. Looking relieved at the secondary nature of his chore, Ross Reed quickly led the mare into the alley. His wife returned gratefully into the bank.

'Mister!' the young girl at the gate called. 'If you been with the Indians, did you see anything of Dad? He and some other men went after a bunch of Apaches.'

'I saw him and he was fine,' the half-breed told her. 'He and the others had the Apaches on the run.'

Francine's smile was even warmer and more grateful than that which Little Fawn had directed at Edge. 'Gee, thanks a lot, mister!' she cried joyfully.

Then turned and ran back into the house, slamming the door behind her. Perhaps to take up again her surveillance at the lighted window.

'I sure hope that wasn't a lie just to make her happy, Edge,' Grace Lutter said grimly as the half-breed crossed the threshold.

'No, ma'am,' he replied, ignoring her husband and the gun now as he moved to the chair at the back of the room where he had sat yesterday: pulled it out from under the table and lowered himself gratefully on to it. 'Sheriff Temple is the only one around tonight.'

'I'll ask the damn questions, woman!' Cass Lutter growled, dropping onto a chair at the table next to where the half-breed sat.

'Oh, do be quiet!' his thin-faced, pock-marked wife countered in a matching tone, reasserting her authority over him now that Edge was disarmed and she was in the secure, familiar surroundings of the store and saloon. Then, as Cass Lutter's face shaded from red to purple as his fury rose, she said to the yawning half-breed: 'Sheriff Temple is the only what?'

He completed the yawn and drawled: 'Cop-out.'

Chapter Twelve

'Without a head you won't have no smart mouth to show off with, mister!' Cass Lutter rasped, angling the shotgun barrels up from the rim of the table to draw a bead on the half-breed's heavily stubbled, dirt-grimed and exhausted-looking face.

His wife, who had moved behind the bar counter, snorted and glared at Lutter. 'If you got nothin' better to do than keep on makin' threats you got no intention to – '

'Hold your friggin' tongue, woman!' her husband yelled, trembling with rage at her but keeping the gun and his eyes fixed upon the face of the half-breed.

'I'm with him, lady,' Edge said, soft and even. Aware that events and Grace Lutter's needling of her husband had pushed the bald-headed man close to the brink of mindless violent retaliation. 'On account of whichever one of you win this argument, I stand to lose most.'

From the way in which the woman fixed the grim expression more firmly into the flesh of her thin face, she seemed about to hurl more scornful words towards her husband.

His finger curled around both triggers of the shotgun was livid – in stark contrast to the high colour of his face.

But then the tension drained out of the woman. And she looked only at Edge – pointedly ignoring her husband. Asked: 'You want a shot of somethin'? Or a beer, maybe? Looks to me like you ain't had the best of times since you left town yesterday.'

'Obliged for a whisky and a beer both,' Edge answered, and shot a wry glance at the less strained-looking Cass Lutter. To add, as he recalled an exchange from the last time he was in the place: 'In different glasses.'

Lutter was on the point of snarling a response. But footfalls sounded on the boardwalk outside and two men turned into the saloon and store. Ross Reed, with boots on bare feet and a sheepskin coat over his nightshirt. And a broad-shouldered, barrel-chested miner, fully dressed in denim work clothes but tousled from recent sleep.

'What's happenin', Cass?' the middle-aged, dull-eyed miner demanded.

Lutter snorted. 'I ain't had no friggin' chance to find out yet, Howie. Cause Grace is wastin' all the friggin' time treatin' this guy like some friggin' returnin' hero.'

The woman banged the glasses down on Edge's table with enough force to slop beer and rye over the rims. The half-breed nodded his thanks and interrupted the rolling of a cigarette to take some coins from a pants pocket and place them away from the pools of liquid.

'Later'll do,' she said and started back for the bar counter. 'Maybe you'll need refills.'

Howie and Reed remained on the threshold, the miner expressing deep confusion.

'Kurt Tuchman saw the stranger ride up the hill, Cass,' the miner muttered. 'But he didn't get me out the sack until he saw the play you made out on the street. What's he done wrong, for frig's sake?'

Edge struck a match on a dry area of tabletop and lit the cigarette.

'Maybe nothin', Mr Royko,' Grace Lutter said. 'Cass is just bein' his usual ornery self.'

Lutter turned his head to the side to spit on the floor without shifting his eyes off Edge's face. The half-breed noted disinterestedly that Howie Royko was carrying a Winchester. While Ross Reed was holding the Spencer and gunbelt picked up from the street.

'I tell you what's wrong,' Lutter growled. 'The other evenin' this guy rode out of town tall in the saddle. Headed south-west after makin' it plain that our trouble was none of his business.'

Tonight he comes ridin' in from the east. No saddle to ride tall in. With an Apache bridle and reins. And the guns he left with traded for a Spencer repeater and a Colt handgun. The kinda weapons that were stole from the army and got to the Apaches.'

'But – ' Royko began, speaking the interruption just ahead of Reed.

'In between him leavin' and comin' back,' Cass Lutter ploughed on resolutely, 'the Indians ambushed the army out on the southwest trail. And all of us heard the message Lee Temple sent back with young Kenny Lewis. It looked like Edge here was mixed up in the ambush and didn't get killed. That Lee was gonna move east on the trail of the Apaches. Since then, nothin'. Until this guy shows up in town again. From the east!'

The dull-eyed Royko nodded several times as Lutter made points. And when the bald-headed man was finished, the miner was convinced: stared accusingly at Edge as the half-breed sipped the rye and chased it with a swallow of beer.

'But there could be a perfectly innocent explanation for all this, Mr Lutter,' Reed insisted, advancing far enough into the big room to place the gunbelt and rifle on a table.

'Cass ain't give Edge a chance to say more than a half-dozen words,' Grace Lutter growled. 'At least young Francine Temple asked – '

'You're the one wastin' time now, woman!' her husband cut in.

'Why would he come back to San Lucas if – ' Reed started.

And this time the half-breed interrupted. 'You said someone named Tuchman saw me come up the hill, feller,' he drawled, looking at Royko. 'That mean you people have just the one sentry posted? And him right here in town?'

Lutter grunted. 'That why you come back, mister? Find out our plans for – '

Edge allowed a sigh to whistle out on a stream of blue tobacco smoke, doused the cigarette in the pool of spilled beer and drove the man with the shotgun into silence with a cold, hard stare.

'All right, feller,' he said into the silence. 'I'll give it to you fast. And just the once. So you all better listen good. Because I don't know how much time we may have.'

He told them. Everything – with the one exception – that had occurred from the moment he was awakened at his night camp beside the trail until he rode back into San Lucas. The only incident he omitted to mention was his recent meeting with Little Fawn.

When he raised the shot glass and took what was left of the rye at a single swallow to signal he was through, Ross Reed was the first to speak. His smile of relief was a match for that on the face of Howie Royko.

'So it really is true, Mr Edge? Lee Temple and his posse have the Apaches running scared. A long way from here.'

Cass Lutter was looking at the half-breed as if he dearly wanted to believe what had been said, but begrudged allowing the benefit of the doubt.

His wife said coldly: 'That Butler sonofabitch! And to think that today you went out to see his whore of a mother and give her a rifle. It's them you oughta be pointin' that scattergun at, you crazy bastard! And usin' it on! Him for what he done to help the savages! And her for breedin' him!'

She snatched a bottle of tequila from the shelf, took off the stopper and sucked a great gulp from the neck. She revealed she was not usually a drinker by her grimace. But she managed not to choke on the fiery liquor.

'I . . . I . . . don't . . . ' Cass Lutter began to stutter. Totally confused.

His wife, her fury expunged by the outburst against the Butlers and the belt from the bottle, looked earnestly at the half-breed.

'You said at the start that maybe we don't have much time?'

Reed and Royko, who had lost their smiles while the woman was lambasting her husband, were now as serious in countenance as Grace Lutter.

Edge told them of his theory about why the Apaches had abandoned the camp at Black Bear Bluff so readily – of their aim to reclaim *El Cerro de Muerto* by making every citizen of San Lucas pay.

'And you figure the Indians have got the beatin' of Lee Temple and the others?' Howie Royko asked morosely.

'They got the whites outnumbered, that's for sure, feller,' Edge replied. 'Whether Acoti was just on the run to get away or had his braves split up into small bands to pick off the posse, I got no way of knowing.'

'Shit!' Cass Lutter groaned, and got up from the table abruptly, allowing the shotgun to hang loosely at his side, aimed at the floor. 'If they done that, we already lost our best men.'

'Something else to tell you, feller,' Edge said levelly.

The woman and three men looked at him, their anxiety mounting by the moment. He finished his beer before he said: 'If you point a gun at me again, kill me. You don't, I'll kill you.'

For a stretched second, the bald-headed man was close to being gripped by a renewed rage. But his fear of the Apaches proved to be more powerful than his resentment towards Edge.

For the same period, Edge's mind was visited by a vivid image. Of a time, long ago, when he had pointed what he thought was an unloaded gun at somebody. He was just a kid. His brother Jamie was younger. Jamie had a tragically short life. And had to live most of it with a crippled leg because the gun had a bullet in the breech.

'Hell, mister!' Lutter groaned. 'You gotta admit I had cause to be anxious about why you come back here? After you stopped us stringin' up them three Apaches the army caught.'

'And you got egg all over your ugly face!' his wife countered. 'Because he come back to warn us about the savages.'

'That, too,' Edge said wearily, as he got to his feet. And became the centre of fraught attention again. 'Need gear for my horse. Some blankets and supplies for the trail. Happy enough with the Army Colt. Like to trade the Spencer for a Winchester. Or buy one.'

Grace Lutter nodded. 'Between us and Bob Sweeney who sells more than just minin' tools, we can supply what you need, Edge. But you ain't figurin' on ridin' out tonight, are you?'

'Like everyone keeps pointing out, ma'am, the trouble around here ain't none of my business. Like to be long gone before anything else happens to force me to take an interest.'

'But you're near done in, Edge,' she said.

Reed added: 'And that mount of yours needs to be rested, mister.'

'And maybe that story you just told us won't sound so good if you take off,' Howie Royko growled suspiciously.

'The hell with that, Howie!' Cass Lutter snapped and there was obviously no subterfuge in his attitude – he was fully convinced that the half-breed had told it like it happened. 'We got to believe him and we got to organise ourselves in case Temple and the boys don't get back here. And like Edge says, this ain't his fight.'

'And we sure as hell ain't done one little thing to make him feel he wants to help us,' Grace Lutter muttered. She looked at the bottle of tequila as if she was considering another drink. But she resisted the impulse.

Hoofbeats sounded. Coming from a distance. Several animals. Approaching the town through the fold in the hills to the south-east. Shod horses.

A man shouted something. From the foot of *El Cerro de Muerto.*

'That's Kurt!' Royko blurted.

'What's he say?' Lutter demanded.

His footfalls, those of his wife and Reed and Royko as they all converged on the doorway – plus the beat of hooves – masked another shout from the bottom of the hill.

'It's Dad and the others!' Francine Temple yelled and her voice – shrill in tone and closer at hand – sounded clearly.

Edge reached the table where Reed had left the guns and he buckled on the belt and started to tie the thong around his thigh.

'How many you see, Howie?' Lutter asked.

'At least four, Cass. Maybe six or seven.'

'They sure are ridin' hard.'

'My God, the others must be . . . '

The volume of sound had been rising fast and the rest of what Grace Lutter gasped was lost under the beat of hooves, snorting of animals and yells of men. As the depleted posse broke from their headlong race up the slope and skidded to a dust-raising halt on the street.

'Dad, you're hurt!' Francine screamed.

'Just a scratch, honey!' her father answered breathlessly.

'But the others, they all – ' Mel Rubinger yelled.

'What happened to them?' From Ross Reed.

'They're dead, ain't they?' Grace Lutter said dully and her pronouncement brought silence except for the heavy breathing

110

of men and horses and the scrape of boot leather as she led her husband, Reed and Royko across the boardwalk and on to the street.

'Ernie Noble, Bob Sweeney, Lipner, young Dargan, Borowsky.' Now there was just the breath being sucked into and expelled through the flared nostrils of the sweat-lathered horses to compete with Lee Temple's mournful voice as he listed the death toll of San Lucas citizens. 'Fred Lande, Lorrimer, the Mullen kid – '

'We had the friggin' savages on the friggin' run!' Rubinger interrupted vehemently. 'But the bastards turned the tables on us. The tricky sonsofbitches split up and started in to snipe at us. Like we was friggin' apples in a barrel! And now they're comin' here!'

Another near-silence, as the crowd which had gathered on the other side of the street from the buildings – in the same way as when the army men brought the Apache prisoners to town – became fearfully still.

Broken by the creak of timber as Edge, the Spencer sloped to his left shoulder, stepped across the threshold of the Lutters' place.

Four of the five survivors of the almost twenty-strong posse whirled towards the sound. Gaunt-faced, hollow-eyed, sweat-stained and dust-covered men suffering the shock of bitter defeat and the exhausting effects of a frantic retreat. The two miners let out pent-up breath. Rubinger stared fixedly at the half-breed.

Temple said: 'Damnit to hell, mister, you gave me a start.'

Edge nodded a curt greeting. 'Been best if you'd given me one, feller.'

'Uh?'

'For me,' the half-breed growled with contained anger. 'I'd have been long gone.'

Chapter Thirteen

Chief Acoti led his braves over the brow of the hill east of San Lucas a few minutes after sun-up. With the glaring yellow orb at their backs: its rays lancing down to dazzle the eyes of those who remained on *El Cerro de Muerto* to defend it.

For the preceding two hours, the whites had been aware of the simple battle strategy which the Apaches planned to carry out. For Ross Reed, from his assigned sentry position had seen the Indians approaching the town along the trail through the Hatchet Mountains' foothills. Then after he had summoned Temple and Edge to take a look, all three watched while the Indians pitched temporary camp.

No wickiups were erected on the blind side of the hill from San Lucas. The ponies were hobbled, blankets were spread on the sloping ground, ceremonial fires were lit and the colourfully attired shaman began to assert his spiritual authority over the assembled braves. Which in this pre-battle period took precedence over Acoti's leadership.

War paint was daubed and feathered bonnets were donned. The monotonous beating of several single-head tomtom drums began to vibrate in the night air. So that the whites on *El Cerro de Muerto* in no position to see the Apaches, received confirmation of the firelight and billowing smoke as signs that soon the attack would begin.

Thundercloud and the other two sub-chiefs posted sentries only immediately around the encampment. And no white sentry except for Reed reported seeing Indians on any other side of San Lucas.

112

Thus did the Apaches make their intention clear. They had announced their presence and until such time as they chose to begin the battle – obviously at sun-up from the position of their camp – they would wage a war of nerves on their hated enemies. Then, because they were a relatively small force, insufficient in number to make an encircling move against such a large objective as *El Cerro de Muerto*, they would launch a full-scale attack from out of the sun.

Chief Acoti would be aware that such a plan ran the risk of inviting high casualties. But the hill was a sacred place which every Apache had hungered to reclaim for many years. And to die gloriously in the battle to take it back from the white eyes would be a high honour. Should any war-painted and bonneted brave have doubts of this, they were erased as the moment for battle drew near: by the frenetic beating of the taut hide heads of the tomtoms and the frenzied dancing and chanting of the shaman.

Only Ross Reed witnessed the Apache preliminaries of battle. Lying in a hollow on the brow of the hill, the hair prickling on the nape of his neck and his hands clutching a Winchester slippery with sweat. Terrifyingly aware of the light of the moon and stars losing its intensity as the grey of false and then actual dawn drove back the black of the night. Then dividing his attention between the Apaches and the line of ridges beyond them: willing the leading arc of the rising sun to show. For that would signal his retreat from the lonely hill-top, back to the men who were preparing their defence against the Apaches.

By the time he saw that first sliver of bright yellow, bellied out of the hollow, took the hobbles off his horse and began to gallop, the preparations were complete. After a frantic half-night of work which had begun only a few minutes following the return of the depleted posse. Preparations for a plan of defence which would cost the people of San Lucas dearly. But in terms of property and livelihoods rather than lives – if it was successful.

The half-breed had taken no active part in formulating the plan. For he had no stake in what would inevitably be lost. And his only contribution to the setting-up of the defence was in the form of advice when he was asked.

And the sole decision requiring more than a passing thought he had to make was after he came down from the hill in the east. When he knew that there would be no danger in leaving San Lucas in any other direction except east.

The same opportunity was open, also, to everyone else in town. But when Sheriff Lee Temple made this known to his fellow citizens, no one even hesitated to shout him down against the beat of the Apache drums.

When the disturbance died down, Susan Reed suggested that the women – certainly those with children – should take advantage of the escape route open to Fort Catlow. She got backers for the idea, but no takers. For the Apaches were going to pay for their attack of six months before. And for the men they had killed only yesterday. Everyone was determined to see them pay.

The work done, the preparations made, everybody except for Reed and Howie Royko who was watching to the north, south and west from the top of the hill of dead withdrew into the cover of the row of buildings on San Lucas's only street. Listening to the drums and the chants, aware of the night giving way to day and glancing often to where the banker's horse was hobbled.

There were few words spoken in any of the crowded buildings. One brief exchange was between the half-breed and the lawman while they stood in the open doorway of the Lutters' place.

'You could have left, Edge. No problem.'

'I know, feller.'

'Private reason for staying?'

'No reason for leaving.'

'You're not saying anything.'

'I got nothing to say.'

Both of them continued to show the signs of weariness and hard travel. But neither revealed any inner tension as the war drums maintained the constant, unwavering beat and the smoke of the ceremonial fires drifted across the lightening sky.

Some of the other men were equally calm-looking. Calling upon past experiences of facing up to known dangers. In the war between the States, on frontier forts or perhaps as civilians while they were struggling to survive in isolated outposts before they settled into a community on *El Cerro de Muerto*.

Others, too young to have had such experiences or too old to

114

draw comfort from memories of survival long in the past, sweated and frowned: did not look directly at anyone else or chance the shortest conversations for fear they would reveal the extent of their anxiety.

Every now and then a woman soothed a fretful child. The younger children slept.

When Ross Reed was seen to emerge from his hiding place and run down the slope to his horse there was a shuffling of feet, a creaking of bones and a series of sharp intakes of breath.

The young and tense-faced Kurt Tuchman who stood by the window on the store side of the Lutters' place snarled: 'Frig the stinkin' army!'

Lee Temple, the broken skin on his right side treated and dressed but his shirt still stained with dried blood, shot a withering look towards the twenty-year-old miner.

'The army has always made its position clear, Mr Tuchman!' he snapped.

'If you want out, son,' Grace Lutter called from behind the bar counter, 'there's still time.'

Tuchman grimaced, then looked ashamed and said: 'Sorry, Lee. For Pa and the others.'

Howie Royko, who had started to move at the same time as Reed showed himself, and covered a much shorter distance on foot, came breathlessly into the Lutters' place through the rear door.

'All clear out there, Lee,' he reported.

Temple's thin face showed a tight grin as the banker slowed his horse crossing the street and leapt from the saddle to lead the animal along the alley.

The drums stopped.

In the silence, the small sounds of Reed installing the horse in the stable out back carried into every building.

Edge moved to stand between Rubinger and Cass Lutter at the saloon window as Temple closed the door. Other doors were closed in the other buildings. Last to sound was that at the rear of the Lutters' place as Ross Reed entered, to be greeted with a thankful embrace by his wife.

'Them Apaches gotta be outta their minds,' Mel Rubinger

hissed through teeth clenched around a half-smoked and long dead cigar.

This as the silence beyond the hill to the east was disturbed by the thud of many unshod hooves against the ground.

'No crazier than you people, I figure,' Edge replied as, like every man squinting towards the sun rising above the hill crest, he checked there was a shell in the breech of his rifle. 'Just that they hate you as much as you hate them.'

The Apaches appeared in a long line, reining their ponies to a halt on the top of the hill. Edge was able to pick out Thundercloud and another sub-chief on the right and the third of Acoti's lieutenants to the left. The chief himself would be at the centre of the line, he and perhaps thirty other Indians impossible to see against the dazzlingly bright sun.

But every brave could see the chief, and upon a signal from him, the mounts were heeled into a sudden gallop. The thud of pumping hooves masked by the blood-curdling war whoops which were vented from every Apache throat.

In the Lutters' place, the stage line office, the sheriff's house, the bank and the premises of the dead Bob Sweeney, men and women gasped and trembled. But quickly recovered their composure. Now that the war-painted and shrieking Indians were in sight they were less terrifying. And looking at them, the citizens were able to steel themselves for the effort to extract their revenge. With, in their minds, an image that was as clearly defined as the awesome spectacle of the charging attackers. A vivid memory of Bob Sweeney. Ernie Noble. Young Dargan. Betty Temple and Francine's young brother and sister. Seth Reed. And every other man, woman and child who was buried over the brow of the hill as a result of Apache hate. Maybe a thought was spared, too, for Costello, Hillenbrand, Jaroff and Draper.

There was no hesitating at the bottom of the dip between the hill to the east and *El Cerro de Muerto*. Probably, the speed of the charge increased as Acoti led his braves up the slope of hallowed ground which had been desecrated by avaricious white eyes. Certainly the volume of whooping and shrieking from the braves' gaping mouths got louder.

Then, a moment later, the voicing of hate was counterpointed

116

by the crackle of gunfire. As the Apaches abandoned their reins to control their ponies with knees and heels: so they could use both hands to pump the actions and explode shots from the Spencer repeaters. Aiming at shacks and tents, tunnel entrances and parked wagons.

'Come on, you sonsofbitches,' Mel Rubinger rasped, the teeth around the cigar bared in an evil grin. 'Keep in mind all that crap your holy man preached.'

It wasn't until the blond-haired man with the pot belly said this that Edge realised there was no church in San Lucas. And that during the hours of darkness and dawn, he had seen no one praying for deliverance.

'That's right, Mel,' Cass Lutter growled. 'It's gonna be like takin' candy from a bunch of babies.'

Similar exchanges were taking place throughout every building along the short street. As the vengeance-hungry people of San Lucas savoured the prelude to triumph.

While, further down the slope, the Apache attack lost impetus. As the braves, despite the fanatic fervour filling their minds and whole beings, realised something was wrong.

They had lost the advantage of the sun's dazzling brightness now. And were within rifle range of the whole town. Yet not a single shot had been fired at them. Their own wildly fired bullets hit only the unfeeling ground or equally inanimate and futile man-made targets.

The battle-cries faltered and died: to give way to shouted questions – as ponies were reined to snorting halts. Attitudes of aggression changed to suspicion as heads swung this way and that – eyes raking the surrounding ridges.

Chief Acoti began to stare fixedly at the row of frame buildings under the brow of *El Cerro de Muerto*. One by one and then in groups, his sub-chiefs and his braves followed his example.

Now the sun acted in favour of the whites – its light sparkling and glinting on the windows of the buildings. Making it impossible for the Apaches to see if there were faces peering down at them from behind the panes of glass.

Abruptly, Acoti shouted an order which was passed along the now straggled line of the halted advance. And the braves slid from the backs of their ponies and lunged for the cover of shacks and wagons and mine adits. No shots were fired.

No words were spoken within the buildings.

A selected few men among the whites stepped back from the windows and still-closed doors. Far enough so that they could raise their rifles to their shoulders and take aim. Except for five other men who crouched, ready to wrench open the door of each building, everyone else withdrew to the rear of the rooms.

The advance of the Apaches was now silent and cautious: spurts of speed between areas of cover and then pauses before the next dash. But relentlessly the Indians lengthened the distance between themselves and their abandoned ponies: shortened it towards the one-sided street.

Edge and probably everyone else who waited so silently in cover was aware that the Indians knew the buildings were occupied.

It would have been better if all except those selected as marksmen had left town. But nobody wished to be denied the experience of tasting the sweetness of revenge. And it was impossible to fool such innately intelligent people as Apaches into believing that buildings crowded with blood-lusting enemies were deserted. Not any longer – now that the period of ecstatic frenzy had been exhausted.

So they knew.

Knew that eyes and guns tracked their advance. And perhaps they regretted Chief Acoti's decision to abandon full-scale attack for cautious advance. Which, at close range, made them easier targets for white eyes who were not skilled with weapons.

But they did not make the further mistake of bunching together. Instead, they spread out far across the slope. So that for the final rush towards the buildings they would be able to attack at the front and sides: and some of the braves on the flank could go around the rear.

'Now!' Lee Temple yelled from where he stood beside Kurt Tuchman at the window on the store side of the Lutters' place.

And exploded a shot from his Winchester.

Part of a second later, a fusillade of rifle shots rang out. Accompanied by the shattering of window glass and the crash of opening doors banging against walls.

118

Then it seemed that every sound that had ever been made since the creation of the universe was collected and released to echo just once in the space of no more than three seconds.

Just ten of the shacks on the claims had been prepared. Those closest to the single street. Tightly packed with almost every metal-made item in San Lucas. Pots and pans, stoves, shovels, bedsteads, cutlery, lamps, crowbars and storage drums. Taken from other shacks and from the buildings on the street. Then every grain of blasting powder from Robert Sweeney's place had been divided among the shacks. And finally a bundle of dynamite sticks was fixed to the outside walls of each prepared shack. In sight of the marksmen but hidden to the advancing Apaches until it was too late.

Two marksmen aimed at each bundle. Only one pair had to pump the actions of their repeaters and fire a second time. Probably missed, because by then the top of *El Cerro de Muerto* and everything and everybody on it was trembling and heaving as if at the start of an earthquake.

But the shack disintegrated anyway. Detonated by something which crashed through the air from another explosion. A tongue of flame, a spark or a piece of viciously twisted metal.

Other things were hurled upwards and outwards. Limbs and heads. Hands and feet. Chunks of human meat too mutilated by blast and flame to be identified. Here and there an entire body.

Apaches were not the only casualties. The prepared shacks were too close to the buildings on the street. But because so few of the citizens of San Lucas were skilled with a rifle, this had to be so. To ensure sufficient bullets struck the targets.

Edge threw himself to the floor as soon as he squeezed the trigger. Those without rifles had been instructed to get down before the fusillade was fired. And those who did the firing should have done as the half-breed did.

Many men and women wanted too much to see the Indians pay at the precise moment that the debt was extracted.

Blast blew the broken shards of glass out of the frames. And pieces of twisted metal flew across the street to beat against the walls or find entry through windows and doorways.

A sliver of glass penetrated Rubinger's right eye with enough force to drive through his head and pierce his brain. He died without a sound, a fountain of blood gushing.

Kenny Lewis, in the doorway of the Lutters' place was blown over backwards. He screamed and then became silent in death as a piece of mangled stove burst open his skin and imbedded itself in his intestines.

A woman in the bank was killed solely by the impact of the blast hurling her against a desk and breaking her back.

Screams filled the air which reeked of burnt powder. Screams of those wounded by blast or shrapnel and those who looked upon the injured and the dead.

Then, as the ground ceased to tremble and ears ceased to ring with the force of the explosions, the killing began again.

As the citizens of San Lucas lunged from the buildings and into the billowing black smoke that veiled the street and the area where ten shacks had once stood. Yelling and firing as they ran, on a seek-and-destroy mission against the braves who survived the devastating effects of the whites' main defensive tactic.

Edge did not join the mindless charge through the blinding smoke. Merely watched for a few moments, grimaced when he saw Howie Royko hit in the side of the head by an Apache bullet, then turned and moved away from the window. He paused just once on his way towards the door that gave access to the rooms for rent at the rear of the Lutters' place. To pick up the Winchester of the dead Rubinger and leave the Spencer in exchange.

Grace Lutter was among the group of women who watched him – some of them holding crying children against their skirts. There was no triumph on any of their faces. Most of them were dumb with shock as they stared at him. Perhaps many did not even see him. Maybe could not hear the shouts and the shooting from outside.

'You leavin' now, Edge?'

'Guess so, ma'am.'

'Like all of us soon. Them that are left.'

The half-breed nodded. 'The Apaches were always on the winning side.'

The skinny old woman looked at him in confusion and anger.

As the shooting became sporadic. 'There'll be more of us left than them, mister!'

He halted beside the closed door. 'And like you said, you'll be leaving. The silver lode's all worked out. No reason for you to stay. Or for whites to live here. And it isn't the entire Apache nation that was just wiped out. Those that died will go to the Happy Hunting Ground proudly. They won back the hill for their own kind.'

A woman began to sob. It was the only sound on *El Cerro de Muerto* as, outside, the surviving men of San Lucas surveyed their own and the Apache dead.

In the livery, crowded with horses, Edge's mare stood ready to leave: saddled and with a bedroll in place, the bags bulged with supplies and the canteens filled with water.

Weeping and wailing swelled in volume. As Edge led the mare from the stable and swung up into the saddle, the voice of Cass Lutter cut across the sounds of misery.

'One more has to die, Lee! Let's go get that Indian-lovin' Butler bastard!'

Voices were raised in agreement. The people of San Lucas had not yet expunged their hatred. Lee Temple waited for the noise to subside. Then shouted:

'First, we bury our dead!'

Edge, hidden from all eyes behind the Lutters' place, turned his horse away from the south-west and towards the north-east. The mare vented a low snort.

'Makes no difference to you, little lady,' he murmured, stroking the animal's neck. 'But I figure that while they're opening up new ground, I've got to cover some old.'

Chapter Fourteen

Edge rode around the hill crests and did not look down on the town. He had seen too many battlefields, during the war and afterwards. Large and small. Witnessed enough of death and destruction to last him a lifetime. And was aware that for as long as his life was to last, he would see others.

So he was unaware if anyone in San Lucas saw him and the horse diminish in size and perspective as he moved up to the highest ridge of the surrounding hills and then went from sight on the other side. Certainly no one called out to him.

He rode slow and easy at first – in his habitual ever-watchful manner. Then, down in the desert valley and back on the defined trail between town and the Butler place, he asked the mare for a canter. And the well-rested animal responded with enthusiasm.

He did not see the lone rider trailing him at a great distance until the cluster of buildings showed at the end of the trail. And so it was not for this reason that he had increased his pace. Rather, because he felt he had had enough of this barren and inhospitable part of the country. Was anxious to complete the chore he had set himself and be gone.

Closer to the Butler ranch he sensed watching eyes – but no menace. The door in the early morning shade of the stoop did not creak open until he rode onto the hard-packed earth of the front yard and swung down from the saddle.

'What do you want, mister?' Calvin demanded.

He was dressed in pants and a shirt. There were no boots on his

122

feet. His left arm had not been put back in a sling. His face was clean, but not shaven.

Edge looked back out along the trail. There was still just the one rider coming in. Without haste.

'If you and him brought bottles, you're wastin' your time. Ma's through with all that kinda stuff.'

'Your wife show up, feller?'

The sandy-haired youngster's frown of belligerence slipped a little. 'Yeah. Yeah, Little Fawn made it. She told me about meetin' you. Thanks.'

'They in there? Your Ma and your wife?'

'Sure. Sleepin'. Both of them were dead tired.'

'Then best you wake them up.' Edge jerked a thumb over his shoulder. 'That could be Cass Lutter heading this way. Him or somebody else from San Lucas who figures you're to blame for what the Apaches did to the town this morning.'

'Just one? I can handle just one.'

He turned to go back into the house.

'No, Calvin!' Little Fawn said as the half-breed crossed the threshold. 'Please, no more killing.'

The Apache half-breed girl was coming out of the rear bedroom. Unwashed and dishevelled, just as she had been when Edge last saw her. She still wore the same torn dress and was holding the gap together with one hand.

Her husband ignored her, to lift the Winchester rifle from where it leaned against the wall by one of the armchairs.

Then the door of the other bedroom swung open and Lorna Butler, fisting sleep from her red-rimmed eyes, came out.

'You?' she said to Edge. Then raked her gaze towards her son. 'Cal, what's goin' on?'

'The Apaches hit San Lucas this mornin'. Edge came out to warn us somebody might figure I was to blame. And somebody is sure headin' in on the trail.'

'I say no more killing, mother of my husband,' Little Fawn cried.

The white woman moved fast across the room to snatch up Calvin's Colt Paterson from the shelf between the two armchairs.

'If it is kill or be killed, it's not goin' to be my boy who dies!' she announced coldly.

123

She shot a powerful glance towards her daughter-in-law, made to advance on the threshold where Edge stood: then halted and snapped her head around to stare at Little Fawn. And vent a groan.

The girl had dropped her hand away from the tear in the dress, and the fabric was gaping open. But it was obviously not the sight of the immature swells of the half-exposed breasts which triggered shock through the woman.

'Where . . . ?' she began and made a sound of strangulation. Then cleared her constricted throat to demand: 'Where did you get that pendant, girl?'

Little Fawn, eyes wide and lips gaping, glanced down at the heart-shaped piece of metal which hung on the thong around her neck. Then looked fearfully at Lorna Butler, Calvin and Edge.

'My mother! Please! Why you ask? My mother tell me my father give it for me. On day I am born!'

'Ma, what's wrong?' Calvin croaked.

'Oh, my dear God!' Lorna Butler said, her face wan and her body rigid. 'What have you done, Cal?'

The woman advanced on the girl, who made to shrink back but seemed to be rooted to the spot. Lorna Butler halted, reached out with her free hand, gripped the throng and snapped it with a powerful jerk. Then held the pendant six inches in front of her face and stared at it for a stretched second of silence.

'Ma?' Calvin screamed.

The rider on the trail heard him and demanded a gallop of his horse.

The woman turned just her head away from the girl to stare at Calvin. 'It was mine!' she said stonily, clutching the ornament in a tight fist. 'He said I must have lost it. But I knew he was lyin'. I knew he'd taken it to give to one of his Indian whores!'

'My husband did not give it to me,' said Little Fawn. 'I tell you this. It was my father who – '

'I know!' Lorna Butler shrieked. 'Your father! Who was Calvin's father, too! The child growin' in your womb is by your half-brother!'

Little Fawn raised both hands to her face and clawed at the flesh.

Calvin Butler sagged against the wall.

His mother stood as unmoving as a rock figure. Not even breathing.

Edge turned and stepped out across the stoop as the beanpole-thin Sheriff Lee Temple reined in his horse and slid from the saddle.

'I've come to arrest Cal Butler,' the newcomer announced grimly. 'Convinced the folks back at San Lucas that he should be tried by due process of law.'

The half-breed nodded and swung up into the saddle of the mare. 'You said something at Black Bear Bluff yesterday, feller.'

'I said a lot of things, mister.'

'About liking it best if Cal Butler was alive with a lot of years of suffering ahead of him.'

'So?'

'You got what you wanted.'

'How come?'

It had been silent inside the house for a long time. Abruptly, Little Fawn vented a shrill scream of despair. And then her bare feet beat on the floor in a run.

'Private,' Edge replied to Temple's question. 'Like I told some-body a long time ago – incest is a family affair.'

Little Fawn lunged out onto the stoop, her pretty face made obscenely ugly by the physical expression of mental torment.

Lee Temple fisted a hand around the butt of his Whitney. But it was not the lawman's gun that cracked out a killing shot. Exploded a bullet which took the girl high in the back, left of centre, and sent her sprawling into the inertness of death in the front yard.

'What the . . . ?' Temple started.

'That a rifle or a revolver shot, sheriff?' Edge asked as he turned his horse away from the house.

'What?' the tall, thin lawman asked, totally confused by the speed he had seen and heard events since reaching the house.

Edge spat into the yard. 'There ain't no mystery, feller. You must know the difference. So you can't say you don't have a clue: as to which Butler did it.'

THE END

The George G. Gilman
Appreciation Society

**PLEASE NOTE that
THE GEORGE G. GILMAN
APPRECIATION SOCIETY
will now be operating from
Mr MICHAEL STOTTER,
42 Halstead Road, London, E.11. 2AZ.**

EDGE: TEN THOUSAND DOLLARS, AMERICAN

by George G. Gilman

Second in a new Western series, this story is set South
of the Border where men live miserably and die
violently.

Ten American dollars can keep a family for months.
For ten thousand dollars a man would slit the throat
of his own grandmother.

Edge knows where such a sum is hidden and the bandits
know that he knows. The shadow of death hangs over
them all.

NEW ENGLISH LIBRARY

NEL BESTSELLERS

NEL P.O. BOX 11, FALMOUTH TR10 9EN, CORNWALL

Postage charge:
U.K. Customers. Please allow 25p for the first book plus 10p per copy for each additional book ordered to a maximum charge of £1.05 to cover the cost of postage and packing, in addition to cover price.

B.F.P.O. & Eire. Please allow 25p for the first book plus 10p per copy for the next 8 books, thereafter 5p per book, in addition to cover price.

Overseas Customers. Please allow 40p for the first book plus 12p per copy for each additional book, in addition to cover price.

Please send cheque or postal order (no currency).

Name ....

Address..

....

Title ....

While every effort is made to keep prices steady, it is sometimes necessary to increase prices at short notice. New English Library reserve the right to show on covers and charge new retail prices which may differ from those advertised in the text or elsewhere.